Dermot Bolger

was born in Dublin in 1959. His eight novels include *The Woman's Daughter*, *The Journey Home*, *Father's Music*, *Temptation* and *The Valparaiso Voyage*, all of which are published by Flamingo. A poet and playwright, his work has received many awards, in Ireland and internationally. He has edited many anthologies, including *The Picador Book of Contemporary Irish Fiction* and devised and edited the bestselling collaborative novels, *Finbar's Hotel* and *Ladies' Night at Finbar's Hotel*. Bolger has been an energetic champion of new Irish writers as founder-publisher of Raven Arts Press, which he ran until 1992, whereafter he co-founded and became executive editor of New Island Books. He has been Playwright in Association with The Abbey Theatre, Writer Fellow in Trinity College, Dublin and in 2002 received the inaugural Hennessy Irish Literature Hall of Fame Award.

From the reviews for *The Woman's Daughter*:

'A wild, frothing poetic odyssey, swinging backwards and forwards in time to pick up the stories of other "flukes of biology and chance" – the forgotten people who have lived and will live in the same place, on the outskirts of the "city of the dead".'   *Sunday Telegraph*

'*The Woman's Daughter* is a daring and courageous novel, even an experimental one, and reading it is at times a painful experience. As a peephole into one man's version of the long, dark night of the soul, it will not be bettered for quite a time.'   *Sunday Press*

'Bolger raises his dark angels towards some kind of possible salvation in this brilliantly written novel.'   *Irish Times*

'A dark, erotic novel.'   *Irish Independent*

'Powerful, ambitious and original.'   *...pendent*

DERMOT BOLGER

The Woman's Daughter

Flamingo
An Imprint of HarperCollins*Publishers*

Flamingo
An Imprint of HarperCollins*Publishers*
77–85 Fulham Palace Road,
Hammersmith, London W6 8JB

Flamingo is a registered trade mark of
HarperCollins*Publishers* Limited

www.harpercollins.co.uk

Published by Flamingo 2003
9 8 7 6 5 4 3 2 1

The Woman's Daughter, consisting of Part I and sections of
Part III, was published by the Raven Arts Press 1987
This edition, with new and revised material, first published by
Viking 1991 and in paperback by Penguin 1992

Copyright © Dermot Bolger, 1987, 1991

Dermot Bolger asserts the moral right to be identified as the
author of this work

ISBN 0 00 712120 2

Typeset in Bembo by Palimpsest Book Production Limited,
Polmont, Stirlingshire

Printed and bound in Great Britain by
Clays Ltd, St Ives plc

'Although *finn* strictly means a colour, it is used to designate water that is clear or transparent. In this way is formed the name Finglas from *glais*, a little stream: *Finn-glais* (so written in many old authorities), Crystal Rivulet.'

– Joyce, P. W. (*The Origin and History of Irish Place Names*, Vol. II, 1883)

'But you'll have to ask that same four that named them is always snugging in your barsalooner, saying they're the best relicts of Conal O'Daniel and writing *Finglas Since the Flood*. That'll be some kingly work in progress.'

– Joyce, James (*Finnegans Wake*)

Contents

PART ONE

The Woman's Daughter

There is a city of the dead standing sentinel across from her window. Through the gully between them a swollen rivulet is frothing over smooth rocks brimming with the effervescent waste of factories. Within its boundaries grey slabs of granite are flecked with shards of mud as sheets of rain churn up the black pools that nestle in the webbed tyre tracks. Above its crumbling lanes and avenues stooped ivy-covered trees shiver over the homes where no soul moves.

There is a city of the dead that edges down the grass bank towards her window. To the brink of the rivulet that sprays out from an underground pipe. The gnarled fingers of its railing slot shadows over tombstones from the illuminated carriageway. The holes on the pitch-and-putt course breathe easy without their spears. The alarm on the pub wall waits, broken glass in the car-park dreams of tyres. The last lorry lurches down the steep hill and onward towards the countryside. The bored attendant in the all-night garage cradles his head beside the ranks of switches and dials. The cables and monitors hum in his glass vault, the night's takings snug in the floor safe. He seems to be the only living thing as he lifts his head to gaze across the gleaming forecourt to the railings outlined in the yellow light. Yet even there life stirs invisibly downward. Below the plain stones and pillared crypts that end united in the soil, there comes the inaudible creak of life bursting through. The sigh that is clay capsizing, the bustle of blind creatures being eternally renewed.

There is a city of the dead whose gates all fear to enter. Every morning the woman observes it when she leaves her home. Each evening it stands there, patiently awaiting her return. In the hours between she sits beside the conveyor belt picking the indented cans from the incessant silver stream. At night, when the curtain moves in the room, the moon sketches out the grey stones and rushing water like a sole universe. In daylight the curtain never moves, the room staying in darkness which we have never known.

Would we find a figure there stretched in the blackness? Could it live or breathe? Since the sword of light retreated beneath the door it has lain stationary. What could it dream of, knowing no world beyond these walls, the nightlit river and stones? Food? Light? A Saviour? A trickle of blood? The woman's stories constantly retold?

If our eyes grew accustomed to such darkness we might discern the shape of a nightdress, the outline of a girl and long folds of lank hair. Our ears, still unattuned, hear nothing, yet her head twists towards the door and one elbow lifts her from the bed. Just when we're certain she's been mistaken the key burrows into the stiff lock, the glass panels shiver as the front door slams and the footsteps commence on the stairs. One step, two step, the bogeyman is coming. Three step, four step, your mother is home. The girl's head swings upwards and one bare foot reaches slowly out for the cold lino. The beam of light swarming through the keyhole would catch the white bend of her knee and then be blocked by the key blinking in the lock and the flood of electric light saturating her eyes with a searing whiteness through which the woman came home exhausted from her work.

But it is night now, they should be sleeping according to the ritual played out in that house day after day. The woman returned to her parents' bed, the child silent in her own. Soon it will be time for the woman to rise, a second before the clock would shatter the stillness if not smothered by her hand. She should stand cooking breakfast in the winter dark, two cracked bowls of thick steaming porridge carried up the stairs. Her mind returning to the worry of leaving the house for work, the exhortations for silence, the fable of the man who guards the stairs, the double checking of each lock.

Except that one of them is squatting in a heap beneath the window with the curtain torn down. The single bed is empty, the blankets forming mountain ridges across the floor. She hugs herself as her eyes, terrified, never leave the woman sitting on the chair beside the door that should not be open, above the hallway where the shards of hammered glass glint in the streetlight coming through the broken frame. The night air like an intruder sneaks in, carrying off

5

the stale smell of sweat and urine and polish. The woman lifts her head.

I should never never have let that plumber in. It was him started it all. The first person since those busybodies inside the house for eighteen years. I wouldn't have let him in at all only the Corporation sent him and he refused to go away. The typical sneaky sort he was, asking all sorts of questions.

'I suppose you're lonely here all alone?'

All alone, I ask you! You needn't think that he fooled me for a moment. He was sent by them down the street, always prying around and trying to poke their noses in. Do you remember the trouble I had trying to mend that tank the time the ballcock broke? Balanced up on the ladder stuck in the bathtub in my nightdress with both hands plunged deep into the icy tank trying to do something that would fix it. And the water pouring out into the yard from the overflow pipe up beside the gutter for three days in a thundering fountain that formed a black pool swirling down the drain. A good skirt I wasted trying to block the hole where the water kept rushing into the tank.

And then I came down here and sat beside your bed with my hands all red-raw and numb from the freezing water, and I thought you were asleep until you sat up in the darkness to reach out and begin to blow warm air on my palms and rub them till they started to thaw. There was just the two of us like always, but you were nursing me for a change, and though from the side of the house we could hear the torrent of water splashing down into the yard, we were cut adrift all high and dry like Noah sailing off in his Ark.

I was so happy that night with my hands in yours as if it made up for everything. Because I could have been all sorts of things, you know. I had talent when I was young. In school I used to be in plays in the classroom, and once Kitty Murphy and myself did a sketch for the Christmas show at the Parochial Hall. We were dressed up as cleaning ladies with mops and buckets and curlers in our hair and the whole place roared with laughter. But you know, I wouldn't swap that night for the whole world, with the two of us up here and you leaning forward to blow warm air all over my hands.

But still they'd no right to call in the Corporation. What business was it of theirs if there was water coming down. In the end, I would have found a way to fix it like I always do, or turn the water off from the street with that big metal key that Daddy used to keep in the shed.

He battered at the door like a policeman and I ducked down behind the glass, but he must have seen me for he banged and banged till I ran upstairs and warned you to lie still as I locked your room. Then he was all smiles when I opened the front door.

'Sorry to bother you, Miss O'Connor, but we believe you might have a bit of trouble with your water tank.'

A great big slob he was in his dirty blue overalls with a cigarette perpetually hung between two rows of brown teeth. I let him up into the attic all right, but he was getting no information out of me. I just stared dumb at him the whole time and then watched him from behind the curtains till he drove off in his van.

All alone! This is my house, and my parents' before me, and they'd better learn to respect it. I chased them off with a bread knife the last time they came calling. The tenants' association, the community week, join this, pay that. I know what they were after. You should have seen them run that night when I grabbed the knife, shoving each other out of the gate like their tails were on fire.

The child had to be fed. That was why she had always shrugged her way to the front of the crowd gathered around the clock. That was why each evening she had to be the first to squeeze her card down into the machine and wait for the click. The child had to be fed. The responsibility blotted every other thought out as she hurried down the passageway without time to join the cluster of women chatting as they put on their coats and smoked in the cloakroom. Out through the cars and bikes and noisy groups walking towards the gates and down the long carriageway where the old woods used to be.

All that was left was the secret snake of the rivulet that glinted to her here and there down in the steep gully that ran beside the dairy. A few trees remained with their roots exposed on the steep bank and often from one of these the children would tie a thick rope to one of the high protruding branches and out they would swing, three and four girls and boys at a time, clutching each other as they hung on to the rim of the old tyre suspended from the end of the cord. They screeched as they lurched out through the blue air above the swirling water and when they were carried back it seemed as if they would never reach the crumbling ledge of earth again. Then one of the boys would catch his foot on the exposed root and they would all fall backwards in a tumbling heap of jeans and skirts as fresh pairs of hands grabbed the tyre before it swung out into orbit again.

The woman loved to pause and watch them from the path alongside the carriageway but the child had to be fed and so she hurried on, past the spot where the old woman once sold wafers of ice-cream from her cottage shop on Sunday mornings, and up the steep hill towards the estate. She walked quickly here, with her head to one side, always gazing down as she imagined the gauntlet of eyes behind windows. Often she found herself suppressing the childhood habit of alternating her steps to avoid the cracks in the pavement and she almost ran the final steps to the sanctuary of the doorway. Sunlight ran briefly down the lino her father had laid in the hall and then was caught and flung back as the door closed. She leaned against the glass for a moment in the musty hallway and listened for the first creak of the mattress above her.

Don't stare at me like that, you frighten me with those eyes. They've gone now, I tell you, they'll never harm you. I've always looked after you, you know I always will. Don't move away from me again, come back daughter, come here like you used to, do you remember? Take down your dress and rock in my arms the way you loved to when you were small. And I'll tell you a story; I'll tell you how we came here, me and Johnny and Mammy and Daddy.

We were all up on top of a huge open lorry and Daddy was cursing because he couldn't get the rope to fit around it. There was a crowd of neighbours from Rutland Street gathered around the lorry and he'd bought a bag of Lemon's boiled sweets for all my friends even though it wasn't Saturday. They kept jumping up and waving at me until I felt like a film star, and then Daddy climbed in beside the driver and with a big black puff of smoke we moved off with the children running behind and old Mrs O'Byrne from the same landing leaning out of her window and calling to my mother who was sitting on one of the new chairs.

We drove away up the North Circular Road with Johnny and myself clasping our hands under the chairs to keep from falling off, past Doyle's Corner until we came over Cross Guns Bridge and saw the big flashing lock of the canal at the flour mill where that woman was murdered, and then out past the orphanage where all the boys in short trousers with their hair cropped like convicts raced over to the tall railings to stare at us and shout at Johnny, and then along by the grey stone wall with the towers till we reached the railings of the cemetery. That scared me when I saw it first, with those carved out tombs of priests and bishops just within the walls covering the bones of figures stretched out in stone, and the big crowd of sombre mourners waiting for some hearse. And then we reached the countryside with the big houses set in their own grounds across from the graveyard and the road sweeping down towards the stone bridge with a pub where the wood began.

We swung left there and up that hill where there was a little row of small cottages and a country lane leading down to the back of the dairy. It felt like we were out in Meath or Wicklow. And then the truck swung left again into an uneven road and we had to grip the chairs tight to cling on. And as I swung my head round to see this street with muck and stones from the builders all over the road and every second house still empty, I got so excited I almost cried out with so much space everywhere.

Another crowd gathered when the lorry pulled up, but this time nobody waved to us. Instead the children stared silently from the doorways or called backwards to their parents inside. My father got out and I could see he was angry. He stood looking up at the furniture as if he wanted to bundle it all up under his coat and run inside.

'We should have waited for darkness,' he said, 'to get the stuff into the house.' He carefully avoided the watching eyes as he hauled at the ropes, only intent on trying to save his pride.

My mother was different. She climbed down from the truck and stood there brushing her hands as if every detail of the street was to be savoured like a prize. A neighbouring woman approached her and with a careless wave of her hair she was gone off to drink tea in a kitchen. Some of the children came closer and craned their necks to gaze up.

'Oi, headtheball, where'd ya get the sister?' one boy shouted and they all laughed. Johnny sat with his feet swinging over the edge of the lorry talking to them. He jumped down to join the crowd as they moved off and called to me over his shoulder. But even though I wanted to follow, I stayed there expecting him to turn again or stop and call for me, but he never bothered and they all just ran on with their feet scrambling for a kick at a small plastic ball.

My father and the driver were working without ever exchanging a word, shifting piece after piece of furniture in through the hall door. After a while, the driver stopped as if asserting his independence and offered Daddy a cigarette. They stood in the doorway silently smoking. The winter twilight was coming in, dragging a cold mist down with it.

I walked past them into the hall and climbed the bare stairs to the top step. *This is my step*, I thought, *this is my house.* I said it over and over again as if I couldn't believe that other floors weren't built on top of it and people would not keep tramping up and down to them. And as I sat up there on that floorboard in the darkness, gazing down with a strange sense of pride at the bare circle of light in the hall, it seemed as if a child's bony fingers reached out to pinch my back from the empty landing behind me. I never turned my head, I sat perfectly still, watching the backs of the two men as they bent beneath their loads, and listening to the echo of their boots retreating down the concrete path.

Every morning the same; the monotonous meals prepared and carried upstairs, the silence when they sat, the manic cheerfulness of the woman's voice as she unveiled the small tokens of gossip and snatches of conversation she spends her day inventing to carry home like worms in her beak. And then the irretrievable silence settling like dust in the room when the train of lies slows to a halt and there is nothing left to make of the day. Then sometimes, like now, the story will begin, narrated over and over, part by part, as if some key that had been mislaid in all the other tellings might suddenly glint in the light of this one. Again and again the faces, the actions, the voices of this house, as if the recounting could somehow exorcize them. Always she begins it for the girl whose mute eyes show no recognition. Always she finishes it for herself as if only the chain of memories sustained her.

The sitting-room was always cold, no matter if you lit a fire. You could put a glass of ice beside the heater and it wouldn't melt. At first Johnny would never go upstairs by himself. I'd find him alone in the hall and he'd take my hand even though I was smaller. We'd ascend, step by step, always expecting to find white eyes staring at us through the banisters. And then we'd stand at the top feeling foolish, confronted only by three white doors. At night we often heard the sitting-room door slam, even after Daddy had carefully locked it.

The priest came at dusk in a long black cloak and my arms ached from helping Mammy to scrub the lino clean. We knelt in a circle with beads in our hands while he blessed the house in Latin. He took out a framed picture of the Pope and wrote our details in the slots below it, and we hung it across the room from the Sacred Heart lamp. The sitting-room door never banged any more. It was always kept locked and only used for visitors. Even now, I'm frightened before I open that door, as if Mammy and Daddy are still kneeling there, the beads in their hands criss-crossed by cobwebs.

This is the spot where the archers' horses paused first by the stream. They shook their manes that were caked with mud and lowered their noses towards the water. The King rode past with his lieutenants and stopped to examine the ancient trees which the saint had planted there. Sunlight quivered through the thick foliage and sparkled upon the axes the foreigners carried by their sides. Here where two streams met, a mile from the village, they made their camp in the woods. The axes bit into the trunks, the sap ran over the blade. They fell with a loud crackling of limbs. The beech trees and the yew were sliced and shaped into arrows, the ash was bent into long bows. Campfires flickered through the dense forest where peasants watched from the shelter of bushes. Scouts rode back and forth from the walls of the Pale, rabbits bolted into burrows between the roots of trees.

An archer shivers and cries in his sleep, the friends who bury him catch his inheritance. Plague runs swiftly through the ranks, delirious strangers shiver among brambles and day lilies as they await death. On the hillside above the rivulet, Henry surveys the trench being dug. Clad in mail the bodies tumble down, some of them still breathing. The horsemen ride towards the coast, the peasants come out to stand in the clearing. They run the white shavings of ash and yew between their fingers. A summer breeze blows down from the north, the limbs of the sacred trees bow their heads secretively.

Below the window we could see the stream, but not set in a park like it is now. There were big tangles of bushes and old trees down there, and you could watch it disappear into the meadow that was walled in by the convent. Sometimes after dinner on Sundays, Mammy would cajole Daddy to walk with us down Washerwoman's Hill to the Botanic Gardens. There'd be rows of black bicycles parked outside and crowds walking along the bright avenues of flowers. And the first place we'd always visit would be the huge glasshouses, all dripping wet in the steeping heat with tropical plants reaching up to the sky and water lilies in bloom on the walled pond. But I'd grow impatient and I'd tug at her hand, and drag her out past the sign beside the door forbidding perambulators.

They'd laugh at my haste as I pulled them along, through the old trees and grasses where nobody else went until I came to the wall with the convent. There we could see it again, brown now and sluggish, flowing out of that silent valley where nuns walked. Johnny and I would drop petals in it and walk along, following their progress till it came to a turn where the water banked steeply with a wild spray of foam down a waterfall and sped away. We'd race across the bridge, trying to keep up as the petals bobbed and spun in a white tide, but we could never catch them as they spun away, past the rose garden to escape down through Drumcondra. And every night when Johnny and I lay together in bed, we'd invent all sorts of plans for the future.

Do you know the one dream we always both had? What we both said we'd do when we were big enough? One morning we would set out off up the country and find where the stream first rose from the earth, and then we'd walk every step of its path, down Watery Lane and across the North Road, through the village and down the steep valley through the woods, then past our house and we'd wade into the convent grounds, through the Botanic Gardens and go on down by the parks and the factories, and on and on until we finally came to where it entered the sea. And there we'd stand together like those explorers in that film in the Casino who'd discovered the source of the Nile.

There is a legend of the dead, unboxed and unaccounted for: the story of a hunger spreading across a land. Small cabins caving in and skeletons in rags crawling through the woodland to beg alms from horsemen galloping towards the walled houses beyond Shallon. The year they stripped the carvings from the walls of the ancient reformed church, where the stench of the dead in the crypts beneath the flagstones had begun to sicken their descendants kneeling at prayer. Past the unmarked plot where the cross lay buried since Cromwell, by the gates of Dr Harty's asylum at Farnham where twenty-two opulent incurables ranted, and through the small lane at the rear of the tavern, the chiselled marble carried in procession towards a newly consecrated home.

There are stories with nobody left to remember: of smallpox and cholera secreted in the breath of children panting from mud-hut to famished hovel, and of the headland where two streams met at the forest edge where each evening they laid them hastily, unnumbered and still warm in the open pit outside the forked railings of the cemetery.

There are legends of lights leading to nowhere, of hungers in isolated places that could waste a person. There are spikes and concrete foundations, cables twisting through the vaults beneath floorboards. There are skulls of children smiling upward.

At a quarter to nine every morning, Kitty Murphy would call for me and we would walk together to school. There was a steep bank beside the school wall and a bush that we loved to climb through. Then we'd walk primly up the steps where Sister Carmel was watching in the yard. We were in the middle one of the three classrooms lit by high, narrow windows that could only be opened by pulling long cords. There was a stove in the corner to keep us warm and two quivering tubs of ink in each desk. You'll never know what I saved you from by never letting them get at you.

Each morning I would be hauled up and Sister Carmel would ask me my name. I'd stand in that space in front of the desks where the floorboards glistened with polish and swallow once or twice before I'd say, 'Sandra, Sister.' She'd grab my hand screaming, 'What sort of a mother have you at all!' and I'd feel the pain shoot up my arm like an electric shock. Twice the thin cane would flash and she'd shout, 'What class of a mother gave you a pagan name?' as my other wrist was clenched by her fingers. My hand would not open and the cane cracked against the white knuckles.

'Your name is Brigid, after our saint. Now what is your name?' And all I could think of was that woman waiting for me at home, of how I could hug her in the hall when I escaped from here, and I could never utter the foreign name they wanted. I'd stand silently with the palms of my hands buried under my armpits and the tears streaking down my face as I watched that old, puckered face in the habit staring down at me.

'We'll make you a Christian yet, no girl here will have a pagan name!' Then the cane would dart across my bare legs as I jumped back against the wooden desk and she'd prompt the class to take up the steadily rising chant, 'Brigid, Brigid, your name is Brigid!' All the smug Claires and Marys and Teresas, thankful for the diversion and glad that it wasn't them. And when I finally said, 'Brigid, my name is Brigid,' I knew it was a betrayal of the woman I loved.

At three o'clock the bell would ring and we'd burst out screaming through the gates. The girls would gang up, chanting 'Frigid Brigid! Frigid Brigid!' and follow me and Kitty Murphy to the end of our street. I'd bang on the knocker and throw my arms around her waist, crying with my face buried in her dress, and she'd hug me and cup my face in her hands, smiling as she said, 'What's wrong, Sandra? Were you bad at spelling? Were you bad at sums?'

But what could I say to her? How could I tell her the name she gave me was wrong? So I'd just climb into her lap and clutch her and cry until finally she would grow cross. 'We never had any secrets before,' she'd say, lifting me down from her lap.

I'd set the tea things out on the oilcloth on the kitchen table and my father would come in and wash up after work. They called him *The Doctor* there because he arrived into the factory each morning in a suit with his lunch in a leather bag and changed into his overalls in the toilets. Johnny always seemed to have a fresh cut or bruise that he'd picked up after school, fighting in the Cabra Wars. Then, still clutching a bit of bread and butter and banana in our hands, the pair of us would rush out into the street

and run screeching between the lamp-posts to play Statues
or Relievio or Hide-and-Seek.

I'd stand on the wall with my face pressed against the telegraph pole and count up to thirty before spinning around
to scan the dark gardens with their big rucks of hedges and
walls to make out the shapes of the hidden figures.

And with my skin tingling with excitement and my
breath clouding with the cold I'd forget everything except
those friends dodging in and out of the shadows till morning
came again and Kitty Murphy knocked to accompany me
on another slow journey of fear. What would they have
done to you? How could they have understood? Whatever
else I've taken from you, daughter, at least I've spared
you that.

Climb over the gate below the row of old labourers' cottages
on the slope of the hill. Drop down on to the grass where the
horse's hooves have left their mark. See the mare snort and
quiver as she watches you approach. Two girls advancing
hand in hand towards the nervous animal who turns as they
dart forward with sunlight minting silver from her hooves
and gallops towards the laneway that runs above the dairy
where the old man is watching.

In the glade below the other children call as they run
down towards the sparkling water. Johnny smiles as he
stands with his net, barefoot in the stream, and she is
surprised by how small he looks surrounded by the gangs
of boys. A fish is sighted and they stumble clumsily towards

it, their feet churning up muck through which it vanishes. Midges throb in the blue air, a parent shouts from the road, an older girl lifts up her dress and splashes across an overhung pool.

Summer pours through the twisting branches, the greens and browns mirrored in the stream, and she wishes they were all gone and there was just Johnny and her climbing down across the stones in the direction of the sea. They are all her servants inside her dream world. She lies like a princess on the bank as handmaidens splash around her, and in the evening she will bathe alone in the cool water while two maids wait with the silken cloak they shall drape about her shoulders. Johnny smiles and climbs up beside her. They hold hands, with their bare feet distorted in the water.

Do you know what I hate? I cannot stand to see you lying near the edge of the bed. If you stay in the centre you cannot fall. That's sensible, and sense costs nothing. When I was young I was taught that you always left a space beside you for your guardian angel to rest. She was with you through the day and watched over you at night. I'd sleep with Johnny curled up beside me in a ball and our angels hovered on both sides never needing to rest. We were not supposed to talk but we did, often for hours about anything. Away from the crowd he always seemed bigger with all the wisdom of those two extra years. Often to tease me he'd put his feet up against my stomach and begin to roll me over towards the edge of the bed.

'I'll tell on you, I'll tell, you'll crush my guardian angel,' I'd whisper urgently, and he'd giggle and roll me back to him with his feet. One night when he pushed me, I just seemed to keep rolling like the bed was being pulled down towards the floor. I remember the panic, with his hands trying to grab me and then falling into the black space with no angel there.

It was daylight when I woke in the depths of my parents' bed and when I put my hand up to my head, it throbbed as if the bandage there had been strapped on too tight. It felt like a giant hand that was trying to crush my skull down through the mattress and I kept on screaming until my mother came. She had to lie in beside me to make me stop, just the pair of us in that double bed. And I curled up against her warmth and slept like I have never slept again, in that bed I used to crawl into after waking at night in our old flat. It was like being in the womb again, all black and safe, all loved and warm.

I was alone when I woke next and I could hear noises in the kitchens and backyards all down the row. The sound of people at tea and dogs barking across gardens so that I felt scared and forgotten, alone in the darkness. I wanted her back in there beside me, I screamed and screamed to make her come. And then I heard the creaking footsteps, one, two, three, four, the bogeyman climbing the stairs, only it was my father who opened the door to shout for me to stay quiet and not be disturbing the neighbours. I lay by myself feeling cut off, like Mrs Colgan's retarded son up the street who was kept in the house all day and who I only saw once being chased by his mother when he escaped.

I must have slept again because it was the door opening that woke me and old Mrs Whelan, the nurse from around the corner, came into the room. On the landing I could hear my mother whispering as she sent Johnny out to the shops for biscuits. Mrs Whelan called me a brave little girl and held one hand on my shoulder as she pulled the plaster on the edge of the bandage off with one long tear. After she had bathed and rebandaged the cut and was gone, Johnny was sent up with the rest of the biscuits. He sat on the edge of the bed, apologetic and grateful that I hadn't told on him. But I would never have betrayed him no matter what he did to me. Indeed, the more he would have done, the prouder I would have been to be able to forgive him and prove myself worthy to be his companion. I gave him two of the chocolate biscuits with a kiss and ate the rest in the darkness beneath the blankets. The next morning I woke up in my old bed still clutching the plastic wrapper.

In dreams the bed always seems to slope, the darkness waiting to claim her. Walls observe her climbing the stairs, coat-hangers sway behind stationary doors. Her father brings home a builder who tries to explain the changing temperatures in different rooms. Late one night they are awoken by her mother's cry. Her father runs to the doctor in the next street. He drives the few hundred yards in his car to assert his social position.

She makes her First Communion in a net of white, orange candles weep heavenwards like tears defying gravity, the scrubbed knees of segregated boys gleam from the right-hand pews. She races down the steps towards the *Dublin Evening Mail* photographer, then watches her Saviour being crucified in the darkness of the State cinema, gently rattling the accumulated coins in her small white purse.

After school, Kitty and herself walk stiffly between the Stations of the Cross, with two lace handkerchiefs covering their heads. Kneeling at the grotto in the car-park they swap stories. The man who had raved that there was no God and ran up the aisle of the church without genuflecting, clutching a loaded revolver. And when he fired straight at the tabernacle, the bullet hit it and bounced back right through his heart.

Or the man in the house who'd renounced Christ and found that all the doors were locked. The calendar on the wall had a picture of Christ and that very date marked with a red circle. He tore it off and the next month had the same picture and date marked in red, and the next and the next. They found him dead on the floor with twelve different scenic views of Ireland lying torn from the calendar at his feet.

The wooden hatch slides shut and the mesh of light is gone. She leaves the darkness of the confession box and says her penance kneeling on the stone step of the side altar decked with candles for people's intentions. *Should I die now, my soul would fly straight to Heaven. My guardian angel appear in silver and gold to guide me home.*

I have the scar still under my hair. If I shaved my head you could see it. Somehow, life seemed different afterwards. I began to stammer when asked questions in school. The words stuck like bits of hot coal in my throat. But Johnny was always there to protect me, to shout back at the girls chanting my nickname, to watch me through the wire dividing the two playgrounds. When break was over, the bell would ring and each class would stand to attention in line. The gulls would go mad clawing for bread as we lifted our arms up and down to each command barked in Irish.

Four years ago this Christmas, Kitty Murphy, or Katherine as she calls herself now, came home from England. She called to the door and we both stood there. I couldn't let her in with you upstairs, even though I desperately wanted to trust her. It was hard to believe who she was, thirty-three then like myself, but so sophisticated looking. She has three children now and a husband, a civil servant in Leeds. After a few minutes I just wanted her to go, I became suspicious like I always do. I muttered and stared down at my feet until I drove her off and closed the door. Then I stood in the hall and realized what I had wanted to say, *you're the only friend I have, don't leave me, help me to get out of here.*

I went up to my parents' room and stared in the wardrobe mirror, the same style of clothes I've worn for seventeen years, the hair combed down the same way, that face that had forgotten the feel of make-up, my short podgy figure. I could be any age up to fifty, a curio to be stared at in the street, and behind me I could see Kitty's form in the mirror like a whole life which I had lost out on. I hurt you that night although I didn't mean to, it was just a rage that I could not control. And even afterwards when I had to wash the blood off, never once did you cry out.

Like her, Mr Farrell next door collected boxes. Mrs Smith in the corner shop would hand her down three or four cardboard ones from the high counter and she built a home from them in the back garden, ignoring the jeers of the other girls. Her neighbour's boxes were made of wood and were ranked with wire mesh on the roof of the shed. She stopped inventing her secret world to watch him stand there, his eyes gazing up into the soft blueness of the evening as if awaiting a revelation. She craned her neck heavenwards as the man climbed with quick, aggravated steps on to the shed, and then a speck emerged like a tiny chariot from beneath the single white cloud.

Mr Noonan came out and called, 'You'll win it yet, John,' and she turned to watch him stride down through the cackling hens in his garden. They scuttled in alarm over the brown earth pecked clean, past the apple trees and into the felt-covered hut smeared with white stains on its sides. Finally, one ran too close and he grabbed it by the neck and twisted as Sandra stood in terror. The hen flapped frantically in the air and then swung limp in the man's arm as he hung her from a steel hook on a branch and began to pluck the drifting brown snow of feathers.

The bird seemed to shudder as if not fully dead and he gave her another sharp blow across the neck. The other birds pressed themselves against the fence and cackled, trying to fly into her garden with useless wings.

She turned and ran towards her mother who was holding her side and wincing in the kitchen. She dreamt it for the first time that night, the plucked beheaded body of the bird strutting in the garden where the long worms, red like sticks of rock, slithered out from the hedges to catch her. When she tried to run, her feet would not move and then the child's hand, hard and bony, began to push her forward towards them. She struggled and lost her grip, and down, down she fell until her body jerked awake bathed in sweat against the mattress.

That would always be the sight of death for her, the white pimpled flesh of a headless bird scrambling across the garden.

When I came home from school, the hallway was crammed with neighbours. They went silent as I came in and turned to watch me. I ran quickly through them and found a woman from down the road standing in the kitchen where my mother should have been. 'You poor child,' was all she said, 'you poor child.' One of them tried to put her arms around me and I screamed and broke free, remembering the times my mother had threatened to give me to the gypsies when I was bold. I ran into the backyard thinking that they must have driven her from the house but she wasn't there.

Where was she, I kept wondering, why has she left me alone? Then through the open door I saw Johnny come down the stairs and I ran to him. Daddy was walking behind with his face all red and crumpled, like there was no air left in his cheeks. He shook his head slowly and Mrs Moore and Mrs McCormack began to cry. I could feel tears from Johnny's eyes running on to my face as he held me as though he had fallen and hurt himself. Then Daddy came and put his hands around us both and he was crying too.

A silence seemed to fall in the house and I could only hear hushed voices on the path outside. I started sobbing too because they were all crying and I needed to find my Mammy and ask her what was wrong and why nobody would tell me. Then I realized she must be upstairs, so I broke away from them and ran up the steps two at a time even though somebody tried to stop me.

I opened the door of her room and stopped. Mrs Whelan was sitting beside the bed where a man in a black coat was bent over my mother with his hands on her eyes. 'Leave my Mammy alone, you!' I shouted at him, and when he turned I recognized one of the priests from the village. They both looked at me and I grew afraid to approach the bed.

'Mammy,' I called, and when her head didn't turn I called again louder to wake her. I heard Johnny climb the stairs as I ran over to the bed to shake her. Her eyes were wide open but still she didn't look at me. I felt Mrs Whelan pull me back and say in a low voice, 'Leave her, Sandra, your mother has gone to God.'

I didn't cry then because I knew she was wrong. My mother would never leave me like that without saying goodbye. The person in the bed must be someone else, her sister maybe or a neighbour pretending. I knew my mother would come in the door that evening or tomorrow or the day after, all apologies for being away and that everything would be the same as it ever was because how could life go on without her.

You must understand I was only eight years of age, I knew nothing of death or life. Johnny put his arms around me, and I watched my father give Mrs Whelan two bright, shiny pennies to place over her eyes.

That night, her sister came from England with her two brothers and they gave me money and sweets and called me a brave little girl. It was like a party having them there, with tea and cakes and whiskey, and as I lay in the little camp-bed in the dining-room reading my book, I heard a voice singing from the sitting-room. Later on, I woke up when Johnny climbed into the narrow bunk beside me, because the relations had our bed, and without warning he began to cry again and just went on and on though I tried to tell him that Mammy wasn't really dead, she was just pretending. But he wouldn't stop and turned his back on me so I could feel his shoulders shaking in the darkness until finally I fell asleep with my head pressed against the back of his neck and my fingers pressed in his hand that had reached out to find mine.

'. . . it was on our fourth visit to the house that we finally succeeded in gaining access. Miss O'Connor, who struck us as being very nervous throughout the interview and seemed to be of a somewhat neurotic temperament, opened the door after we had been knocking for fifteen minutes. We had great difficulty in persuading her to allow us into the house.

Finally, having taken our identification cards and examined them for several minutes with the door closed, she opened it again to let us in.

The majority of the furniture and fittings therein seemed to date from the mid sixties and were very worn in appearance although in a clean condition. Miss O'Connor stated that she had lived alone since the death of her father sixteen years previously, and that she had one brother, two years older than her, whose present whereabouts were unknown but whom she believed to be working somewhere in England.

When we explained that the purpose of our visit was to investigate reports from several neighbours who suspected that a second person (whom admittedly, they had never seen) might also be living in the house and could possibly be in need of medical attention, Miss O'Connor again replied that she lived alone. She seemed to indicate, in her own mind at least, that there was some kind of conspiracy against her in the street, and cited some not very coherent examples of this which dated back to the death of her mother in childhood.

At our behest, Miss O'Connor showed us around the house which consisted of two rooms and a kitchen downstairs, and a small bathroom and two bedrooms upstairs. One of the latter was locked, because, as she explained, she had ceased using it several years previously. She tried a number of keys in the lock without success, and then insisted that we return to the kitchen, where a search of various presses yielded up a number of old keys. She asked to be excused while she tried them. A few moments later she returned to inform us that one of these fitted.

The room had thick curtains, was lit by a single naked light bulb and was permeated by a somewhat unpleasant and overpowering smell. It was bare except for a carefully made bed and a single straight-backed chair. There were no personal possessions or items of clothing therein to suggest that it was occupied, although the absence of dust would appear to indicate that Miss O'Connor had spent some time in it recently.

The room, and indeed the whole house, had a rather oppressive atmosphere, and while we found no evidence there of anyone other than Miss O'Connor, we do feel that she is under grave emotional pressure of some sort, possibly rooted in loneliness and/or schizophrenia. Thus, we would recommend some back-up from the Social Services. However, this is outside our jurisdiction and we would suggest that her case be passed on to the relevant section within the department . . .'

My mother was a good woman but she left me in a house of men. When I grew I grew inward in ignorance and fear. The nuns in school were kinder now, but how could you ask them advice or questions? We got a lay teacher the year after that who would take us out on walks.

I loved when she'd bring us through the church grounds and down the main street of the village to the foot of the road into the west. It was like a frontier leading up to new estates named after patriots where gangs of youths were said to roam. Once I was carried up there by the bus and ran down as if caught behind the iron curtain. Miss O'Flynn knocked to get the keys of the graveyard at one of the two old cottages there, and we watched the three Alsatians in the compound beside the steps snarling as they flung themselves against the wire with their teeth bared.

Inside the gates it was overgrown, unlike the cemetery outside our window, with the slabs over old crypts broken in two and faded tombstones lying smothered in weeds. Within the ruins of the ancient church the new shops in the village were framed through the ivy-covered slats where windows used to be. When Miss O'Flynn rang her little bell we all ran through the graveyard towards her, and she'd gather us into a circle around the cross and tell us the story again.

In my mind's eye I could see it as she began to talk, the cross standing, a thousand years ago, at the top of Watery Lane, marking the boundary of the village and the monastery. And remaining there through centuries of nights and days until the curse of Cromwell blighted the land. Whorls of cloud are veiling the moon as the villagers carefully uproot it in the night. The stonemason slowly cuts it in two and the cart covered in straw creaks down the village street in the darkness. A man with a lantern keeps watch from the graveyard steps. I'd imagine myself as a small girl concealed at the back of the silent cluster of watchers as the two gravediggers wait beside the black mound of freshly dug earth. Reverently, as if burying the soul of their village, they lower the twin pieces of stone down into the grave.

Then the conspiracy of silence settles over the village to save the cross from desecration. It is never mentioned again in public as though its name had been erased from their vocabulary. Decades crumble into centuries and nothing is said. In the earth the cloth rots away, worms nose the final threads, the stone returns naked to its first love-bed. It no longer exists, except as a secret in the mind of the oldest man in the village, who received it in a whisper on his father's deathbed.

Then I'd imagine myself again as a small girl just before the turn of the century. I'm laying flowers on a grave in the spring sunshine when the old man walking on two sticks enters with the rector. Matthew, Miss O'Flynn said his name was. He never hesitates for a moment. Slowly but steadily he shuffles over to a sward of grass in one corner, indistinguishable from any other, and bangs his stick down on the spot. Finally the words kept unuttered for centuries are spoken. Like a man yielding up his life's purpose Matthew stares at the rector's face and proclaims, 'The Neather Cross is buried here.'

The rector doesn't know whether the old man is doting

or if he should believe him. Still he is afraid to move from the spot. He commands the verger, whom the old man has insisted must remain outside the gate, to fetch some men with shovels from the fields. I'm hidden behind an old tombstone watching the pair of them who never speak as they wait for the men. The rector rubs his hands nervously together while the old man rests on his sticks, confident and yet seeming to tire as though the life force was draining from him. His face is dark, strong-boned, his features the same as the man I always imagine two centuries before holding the lantern for the two gravediggers in the dark, the same as old Turlough down in Watery Lane whose cottage is the only one left standing in the hollow now.

A man called McEvoy brings a spade from the cottages nearby and another man joins him from the fields beside the wood. There is no sound in the graveyard except the soft incision of spades into the soil, until after half an hour the clank of steel striking stone rings out, sharp as a cry fresh from the womb. Carefully they scrape the clay from the top of the stone until the worn ancient carvings are revealed once more in the light. The rector and the two men examine them excitedly, only I notice old Matthew walking slowly away.

These days when I cross the huge metal bridge above the carriageway that roars down through where the wood used to be, I pause above the ruins to examine the cross. It's forgotten now of course, nobody here is interested in those things. On Sundays I climb those steps and stare in through the railings, but when I gaze at it I never imagine I'm that little girl any more, watching the swinging lantern or the shovels glinting in the sunlight. I think that the pair of us are that cross buried somewhere in the earth and maybe only still alive in somebody's mind. We're waiting here in the darkness for him to find us, like a splintered stone that needs to be set together again.

The street riddled with porches and extensions. Hedges are gone now, front gardens cemented for cars. The top windows overlook the cemetery and the rivulet joining the Tolka beneath a new bridge. One house is grown derelict. Two women wait inside it in the hours before dawn, one huddled on the cold lino beneath the torn curtain, the other leaning forward on the single chair, her fingers constantly intertwining. One speaks in a low voice, urgent but indistinct, one stares back as if not listening and living only in her own thoughts.

Everyone was talking about him in school then. How he stayed there for three days buried alive in his coffin. There was a tube leading down into the earth through which he was able to breathe, and he had taken along books like *Dracula* to read. I couldn't understand anyone wanting to stay down there. For three nights the pair of us stood at that window, thinking of him breathing out there alone among those ranks of crosses, surrounded by decomposing bodies. His picture was in the paper when he broke the world record, clutching a bottle of champagne with the cemetery railings behind him. But I could not get him out of my mind.

To frighten me one night Johnny told me stories, corpses dug up with splinters of wood crushed beneath their fingernails, and shattered teeth smeared with blood where they had tried to bite into the lid. I had a new dream now at night, the coffin is being screwed down and I am unable to move my head or cry out to them. I keep beseeching them to notice the terror in my eyes, but they talk on sorrowfully among themselves as they box me in.

I'd scream and scream awake and Daddy would come in. He'd put his arms around me and say, 'Mammy is with the angels now.' But my fear was so embedded that I was afraid to tell him, as if even to speak those words would make them come true.

At the end of the long gardens the hedgerows began, huge rucks of branches and leaves that one could crawl underneath, and there in a nest of dried leaves it was like a submerged cavern. Three or four bodies could climb inside and play their games in the secretive hedgelight. One boy always lay with his head outside, watching the row of kitchen doors for danger. Johnny would vanish there now and refuse to bring her. She'd watch him wiggle inside from an upstairs window. He'd grow silent when she questioned him, in the darkness of their room.

One summer morning she followed him down, creeping

through a neighbour's garden so as not to be seen. She lay on the far side of the hedge, stealthily pushing aside branches to peer through. Three boys squatted naked by the light of a small candle, their hairless bodies shockingly white in the light. Johnny's face was turned towards her, his body excited as he watched his two companions begin to rub their buttocks together. The twigs snapped beneath her fingers, the naked boys anxiously grabbed their short trousers. As she turned to flee the look-out raced round the hedge to catch her and push her struggling down the leafy tunnel.

'Spy,' one of the boys shouted, 'you were spying on us!' Johnny dressed himself, white faced and ashamed. 'What will we do with her?' one of the others asked, and the boy paused and replied, 'If she saw us, she must take her clothes off and take the oath to become part of our club.'

She started crying as she squatted here, surrounded by them, and it was Johnny who took her hand and said, 'Leave her alone, we're going home now.' He led her out into the fresh air, beyond the gardens, and they walked down silently to where the rivulet glinted between trees. 'What were you doing?' she finally asked, and he threw a stone into the water and said, 'It was a game.'

He sat on the bank beside her and went on: 'It was a club. We swore loyalty to each other. We'd each make up tests of courage and have no secrets between us.'

The pair of them climb upstream over the rocks. By the green light of an overhung pool they kneel down and swear secret faith and loyalty to the *Joh-dras*. He carefully plucks the leaf of a wild nettle and they solemnly give each other a single sting on the white exposed skin of their buttocks, the badge of courage, of blood brother and sister against the world.

Daddy wore his mourning quietly, as if his grief was a stigma that could never be revealed in public. I always seemed to be sitting in the living-room with my homework, listening to his slow desperate pacing of the floor above. We more or less had the run of the house and he would never say a word, but his presence and his grief was always there as though accusing us. Everything I did was done to please him as if I carried guilt around on my shoulders. It seemed like he was balanced on an invisible window-ledge and one mistake or wrong word would push him off.

Three times a week he caught two buses to the scorched earth of Mount Jerome cemetery and every other evening went walking by himself. After tea he worked in rubber boots in the garden, manicuring the lawn as if he could only speak through its ordered shape. It was only when we went out that he'd grow stern, checking our clothes and nails to show the road that he could cope. Often when I played on the street I'd sense him watching from behind the curtains to make sure that I wouldn't let him down, and afterwards, at supper, he'd quiz me slyly about things neighbours might have said to their children.

He never went back to the street where he was born, to the two rooms we had lived on in after his mother's death until we moved here. The friends I remember calling to see him in the flat were never mentioned. His life before this place seemed something sordid to be locked away.

There was an election called then, and when I walked to school men were clambering up ladders to stick posters on every pole. Cars toured the street with loudspeakers. It was the first time I saw Daddy bring people into the house that used to be full when my mother was here. A poster was stuck in every window, and each night two men called for him with bundles of printed leaflets. He'd be cross if he found Johnny and me playing with them, he'd hoard them to his chest like money.

One day I found a torn Labour poster like a fallen leaf on the pavement. I loved its design of stars and red colour. When I brought it home he almost struck me, as if I had carried an ikon of the Antichrist into a cathedral. When the election was over the men never called, the energy of those few weeks seemed to drain from him. On Saturday when he took us shopping into town, he stood reverently aside to let the former schoolteacher, now a Dáil deputy, stride by without returning his respectful salute.

Every year it never seemed it would come until it was suddenly there. The buses throbbing outside the gates as the girls march up the steps in their Sunday clothes. At Tara or Clonmacnois they are lectured on the historical sites, and then the nun claps her hands for them to scamper down the gravel path towards the tiny shop where crisps and toffees and chocolate are drowned in a sea of hands. On the way home they travel, exhausted, through the alien green landscape. There is a fight for window seats and the girl beside her leans over to be sick. Spilt milk is souring in the heat. They sing in the queasy smell of the summer evening.

The morning before fifth class breaks up, with Miss O'Flynn at their head, they parade through the empty streets towards the countryside. The dark-skinned old man watches from his cottage wall beneath the roadway as they pass the red barn and start to move through the fields. Loose gravel sprays beneath their rubber soles, they point out the farms where there is work in the autumn. Some of the girls hold hands and sing, *Now she won't buy me – A rubber dolly!* At Pass-If-You-Can they turn up the hill where the flooded quarry glistens blue in the light. A girl winks at friends and turns to Sandra.

'My brother was swimming in there once and he saw two sharks.'

Her wide eyes gaze out at the water and back to their straight faces.

'And there's a hidden tunnel since the Penal Days from the castle to the old graveyard in the village.'

Girls whisper behind them, 'Listen, they're winding mad Brigid up.' Cows graze in the castle grounds as they climb the curving stairs to the battlements. Her throat is parched from the walk, the blouse stuck to her with sweat. She stares out at the countryside divided up into squares of colour, the blue tar glinting between trees, the outskirts of the city three miles distant. The breeze is fresh against her face as her head starts to spin at that height like a hermit in the desert being tempted by a vision of the world.

I always promised myself afterwards that it would be the last time. I was so resolute that it seemed nothing he could do in the future would break my grip. I remember how the moonlight would slant into the room and I'd lie here occasionally hearing footsteps. I'd think anyone out at that time of night must be embarked on some sort of adventure. Johnny would be curled up back in his pyjamas beside me with his body so hot it was like a furnace to touch. He always fell asleep immediately afterwards, mumbling a few words as he untangled himself and turned to the wall. It wasn't long after my eleventh birthday, and I'd think of our two guardian angels hovering, wounded and disappointed, on both sides of the bed.

Daddy thought nothing of us sharing the one bed, especially after the nightmares I used to have. It was as a badge of courage that I'd first undressed, like as in all the other games of dares. Johnny'd saved up his pocket money to buy a packet of birthday candles. He'd light one on the dressing-table to make it exciting. In the half light it was just like those old games of marriage. I'd imagine him as my husband coming home tired from work. In the darkness it was more sinister, his actions more frightening, more like a stranger. One step, two step, the bogeyman is coming, his hands pushing mine downwards towards that hard and slippery thing. I'd enjoy the excitement then, his breath coming fast against my ear, his hands never still.

It was afterwards that I'd lie awake, knowing that what I was doing was wrong, and terrified that there might be some way for people to guess my sin. I'd think of my father in the next room, how his face would crumble in if he ever knew. I knew that I had let him down, and grew more guarded now and withdrawn in school.

The single candle is stuck with wax on to the top of the chipped dresser. Its small flame lengthens and draws in the shadows along the walls of the room. They lie curled together against the cool sheet below and the rough warmth of blankets above, her feet drawn up into his stomach as she allows him to peel each nail of her toes, just the scratch of nail cutting through nail filling the silence. Then the light clicks in their father's room and they pause for a few moments before they tentatively begin.

The blankets are tossed down below their knees, her nightdress slipped up above her head. His hand stroking across her thigh, he suppresses her giggles with his lips. Both close their eyes, retreat into their separate illicit fantasies – *her husband coming home to her from work* – he draws her hand down to the rigid penis – *his own girl in a doorway down the dark side entrance of the Casino* – where the first light hairs cluster around its base. Stiff with the thrill of fear and excitement they lie, afraid to creak the bed springs, until he grimaces in his cramped position, his mouth pushed into her hair to stifle the panting as his limbs overspill with pleasure.

She watches the white stains settle over her naked stomach, feels his body relax as he turns and drifts towards sleep. The cloth is tucked beneath the mattress, she shivers as she wipes herself, the husband's knock, his bicycle ticking down towards the shed, the first kiss on her lips in the sparkling kitchen, all gone, all gone.

We were in a classroom in the cellars of the church, down a granite flight of steps. The windows had thick hammered panes of glass and so the light had to be left on all day. Every morning I was sent up to the big school with another girl to fetch the crate of Government milk. We'd feel so important that last year to be let out alone, walking through the scraps of bread after break in the concrete yard where the seagulls swooped and clawed at each other. In winter the milk would often freeze, and when you raised the half pint to your lips you'd suddenly swallow raw chunks of ice.

Miss O'Flynn frequently switched into Irish and the whole class would keep our heads down because we couldn't understand what was being said. The times I loved best were the singing lessons, when she would unzip the small fur-lined bag and produce her green-and-cream Melodica with keys like a miniature piano. She'd blow the dust from it with a single shrill note and arrange us in rows against the back wall to accompany us through every hymn in our song book, *Mother of Christ, Star of the sea, Pray for the wanderer, Pray for me*. Those lovely and lonely words sung over and over to her methodic accompaniment till we had them perfect. I felt such joy and safety in being part of a group, a unified voice wafting up into the church where I imagined the women who had come to pray were listening to our singing coming faintly through the floor.

At three o'clock when the bell rang the class would burst out into the tiny passageway, fighting to be the first to crest the stone steps before scattering off in every direction. I would delay until I thought nobody was watching and then slip through the ornate wooden doors of the church. In the porch a stone staircase twisted upward like in a castle to the high balcony where the choir sat. Beside it a wire rack displayed small pamphlets on the lives of the saints and the dangers of marriage outside the fold. Just inside the inner doors there were two small altars with statues and a twisting metal candlestand. Old women always knelt there, whispering loud indistinguishable prayers.

I'd genuflect with my head covered and walk to the top of the church where the two side aisles were always empty. The left one would be drowned in deep shadows and the right transfixed by afternoon light igniting the coloured squares of stained glass.

All alone in that mesh of light I'd pray, trying to recapture the holiness and union with God that I once used to feel. But though I tried to prevent them, my eyes would always stray up towards those white marble limbs of the crucified

Saviour on his cross that would remind me of Johnny's ivory white body against mine in those sessions I had failed to end, and the shame and guilt would rush in.

Those blood-stained eyes stared mournfully down at me from beneath the crown of thorns as I knelt, tiny and insignificant, in the third row from the end, and I knew that unless I confessed my soul was damned. Yet every fortnight when I entered that black box with rows of impatient classmates waiting outside and Miss O'Flynn overseeing it all, how could I begin to tell the bored voice on the lit side of the grille the sins of touch from the night-time and the blasphemy of sight on those despairing afternoons? I'd emerge doubly condemned for the sin of false confession, cast out by fear from my second family until Johnny's was the only company I could still fit within.

johnny johnny hung on the church wall. johnny johnny had a great fall. all the king's horses turned bright red, when mammy loved johnny johnny in bed. always the same, story the same, school and job, and death and pain. we know every word by heart, but when she leaves our fun will start. frightened by that open door, let in the bogeyman from the stair. must stay quiet, must not speak, till mammy mammy is down the street.

I suppose Johnny was always just weak, although I never recognized it then. A few years later on I remember catching a glimpse of him one night in the National

Ballroom in town. We had gone off to see the Clipper Carlton Showband but couldn't get in, so we'd wound up there without him knowing it. I was standing up near the stage to gaze at the Mighty Avons when I saw him hovering in front of a girl with a stiff beehive, trying to work up the courage to ask her to dance.

He was so slow and obviously nervous that her friends began to giggle in the chairs beside her and she became embarrassed. Then he asked her in a rush and seemed almost relieved when she snubbed him and he could merge back into the crowd as if it had been the high point of his night.

But back when I was eleven or twelve he was a hero because, even though he was bigger, he never looked down on me and I felt important and wanted in his company. Besides, I was at an age to want to know and there was nobody else to tell me things. Poor Johnny, always laughing and joking when we were alone, and then quiet in company like you'd think he was in bad humour till you realized he lacked a single shred of confidence. Always tucked up in the centre of a crowd of lads as if living off their collective bravado. For all his air of knowledge I suppose he knew as little as I did in those days.

Stillness reigns when the key is turned in the lock. The woman's footsteps turn to descend the stairs, pausing every morning to listen for sounds before the glass rattles in the panel of the front door as it is slammed shut. The noise reverberates through the floorboards up into the dark room where the girl lies, and all the glass there seems to take up the echo and quiver until the very air is vibrating with sound. She never moves from the mattress, but beneath her closed eyelids she can feel the roof descend. Walls advance and begin to spin as the bed springs undulate like a rippling tide. Breathless with excitement, she waits for her friend to visit her.

He calls her name through clanging coat-hangers, there is no danger – she can answer him. He is both older and younger than her. He has no age. He has lived forever. He tears apart all the colours that form black; dissolving reds and blues spin in glowing bands around the room. Nothing there is stationary any longer, he breathes his life into the woodwormed furniture. And nobody can reach her inside that cocoon, she is deaf to the shouts of children playing outside. She never has to warn him when to leave, johnny johnny knows when his time is done. He knows that he can never be forgiven, he knows he must remain her secret lover. Slowly he gathers himself up, softly the bed springs are reined in. Only darkness remains in the room when the girl's eyes flicker open and the woman's footsteps come.

After tea one evening I began to get cramps as I was washing up. It was like a dull sharp pain that would never end. I climbed up to this room and lay on the bed frightened to call for help. When I ran my hand gingerly up along the inside of my dress my fingers were smeared with blood. I was sure it was the consequence of the deeds I had committed with Johnny, our secret finally being made public.

The blood seeped out until I thought I was about to die. Johnny came into the room looking for something and stood staring at the stains of blood where my hand touched the coverlet. I wouldn't let him touch me or tell him what was wrong, so he shouted down to my father who fidgeted awkwardly at the foot of the bed. Embarrassed, he pushed Johnny out of the room, told me to lie still and left me alone.

For ten minutes I waited, listening to the stillness of the house and then Mrs Whelan arrived, still in her nurse's uniform, and took my hand. She cleaned me up and dried my tears, and sat beside my bed for two hours talking and teaching me the names of things.

'I'm only around the corner from you, Sandra,' she said, 'you know if you are ever worried you can come to me.' For a moment I almost told her everything and then I stopped, afraid to lose her esteem.

'I'll be okay, thank you,' was all I said, and she smiled back as she left the room. Johnny came up when she was gone and began to take spare blankets from inside the wardrobe. He said Daddy had told him to sleep on the sitting-room sofa until he had time to buy a single bed for downstairs. He paused as he told me and stood at the door with the pile of bedclothes in his arms. I know he wanted to say something but for the first time in our lives there seemed nothing more to say. I turned on my side away from him and heard him click out the light and reluctantly close the door of this room on himself.

Without him the bed was empty and huge. Alone for the first time in its depths I listened to the footsteps on the pavement outside and this time I knew where they were all going as if the innocence of my childhood had been washed away now that I was a grown-up woman of thirteen.

Stately as an ancient courtier, the retarded man with the stick bids her enter the peeling gates. Every Sunday afternoon since she was a child he has stood sentry at the entrance to the lane between the church and the school. This is where she comes to be alone on the Sabbath when all the shops in the village are closed. Nobody lives on the main street any more, the car-park of the vast, guarded shopping centre covers the site of the last few cottages and the post office. Graffiti on the high walls of the lane proclaim Bob Marley's immortality, lovers pledge themselves with aerospray cans and illicit armies canvass support. She turns to watch him run his stick against the bars of the gate and behind him sees the figure of Turlough approaching.

The gaunt old man stares at her like the guardian of her childhood. She feels safe when he watches her as if somehow Turlough knew every secret of her life and yet did not condemn. The weekends are the worst for loneliness, the deserted main street, the empty playground beyond the wall, all reinforce her isolation. Only the lonely, withered figure of Turlough, who never speaks, seems to recognize her, seems to tell her that she is not alone in her story, that she is part of something greater, that there are others as abandoned as her.

For some reason his eyes always bring her solace as they stare at each other, while the shambling retarded figure between them smiles as he twirls his stick against the bars, lost inside his private nightmare.

Won't you even move a little closer to me? Rise up from the floor and get back into bed? I could make you cosy if you only tried. Remember I'm your mother, I want to look after you. Will I tell you the first joke I ever heard?

'Will I tell you a joke – a bar of soap! Will I tell you another – a pound of sugar!'

I suppose they're silly, but we used to laugh at them when we were small. Do you know what I'll tell you? I'll tell you my first job, you'll like that.

We were the biggest class in school and that summer we had to sit our primary exam. We never raced around the playground like the smaller girls now, we huddled together in the open shed laughing at jokes we were afraid to show we didn't understand. One girl kept watch to see who the boys, pressing themselves against the wire and wolf-whistling, were staring at, while the rest of us pretended to ignore them.

The McCormack twins always smelt of fish because they were already helping their mother who worked an evening shift at the processing plant. We'd tell each other the jobs we all wanted to get and sympathize with the two girls whose parents had the money to put them into secondary school.

On the last day the Head Nun came down the steps into the cellar to make a speech. She called us a credit to the school and hoped that what we had learnt would always stand us in good stead. There was a wide world beyond this classroom and though we would not notice the years flying till we had children of our own, whether here or in England, we'd still always be her little girls.

We gave three cheers for the nun and three cheers for Miss O'Flynn, and presented her with a box of milk chocolates that she shared out amongst us. The nun led us in a final prayer and reminded us that faith was the most precious gift we would ever receive before opening the door for us to file out into the summer light.

For the last time I walked up those steps with Kitty Murphy, our arms entwined, and we imagined ourselves in just a few years standing at the gates of this very school, leading our own children down to enrol, and how we'd laugh about old times with the familiar figures smiling in their black hoods. We paused at the corner to embrace and moved off like blood sisters with the wetness of her tears mingling into my own as they rolled slowly down my cheeks.

The smell of lacquer always clung to her clothes and hands even though she scrubbed them for hours each night. In the hot stifled atmosphere of the salon she brushes up the piles of shorn hair from the floor to be packed into boxes and sold to wig manufacturers. She trains her hand to be steady as she pours the cheap lotions into expensive jars for resale, and her feet ache as she runs from chair to chair, setting out clean towels and combs while the customers gaze at magazines from beneath the whirling dryers.

Autumn sunlight flashes against the windows of the buses in the street below the cramped rooms where meekly she obeys the commands of every member of the staff who, on her one half-hour break in the day, introduce her to the alien taste of coffee and allow her to marvel at the colour pictures in the pile of English women's magazines.

Of course, I gave my wages every week to Daddy and from it he'd give me pocket money. In the evenings after work I could go walking in the street because I was free from homework. The films in the Casino were now becoming over-sixteens and I loved to watch the couples queuing there for the evening show.

It was only a matter of time before a boy would come along and at first, I'd be coy but finally I'd agree. He'd pay us into the 2/6d seats where I would let him take my hand, and afterwards he'd offer to walk me home and we'd take the dark side of the main road, over beside the stream and the trees on the bank, and he'd hold me against a trunk to press his lips on to mine.

After a few minutes I'd protest and he would stand back to apologize. I would give him my hand as we'd step again on to the path and when he left me at the gate, I would rush into the dark sitting-room to watch him standing across the street maintaining a lonely vigil beneath the lamp-post.

I'd go to bed, and all those memories of Johnny would be banished as I'd fall asleep dreaming of that young man out there waiting for me. But no boy ever asked and I'd never have been allowed to be seen on the street in such company. The door would be locked on me at nine o'clock and no amount of pleading would get me back in.

Acne and bristles and cigarettes. Johnny rarely stays at home now. Each evening he merges into a gang of mates, shouting from the open platforms of dark green buses. In the Astor, they wolf-whistle Brigitte Bardot in *A Very Private Affair*. In the Bohemian, *Rock Around the Clock* is being revived. They spend hours sharpening the tips of steel combs to rip out the seats during the theme song.

In the twisting streets around Stonybatter, small pubs welcome the scrum of under-age boys. At weekends they spend most of their wages there and queue in the greasy fish and chip shops of Phibsborough before strutting the two miles out by the cemetery with catcalls at the couples walking home from dances. They piss in front gardens, ring doorbells and empty dustbins along the main road. She hears him come in at two o'clock in the morning and waits for the light switch to click off in her father's room.

On Friday nights, voices are raised in the kitchen as he demands Johnny's wage packet, and when Johnny has stormed óut, slamming the front door, her father comes in to her with his face white in the first shock of defeat. They sit in the chairs on both sides of the fire with only the flames and the red lamp in the corner to light the room, and listen to the voices on Radio Eireann, the farming reports, and whine of accordions and asthmatic tin whistles in strict and monotonous three-four time filling up the silent room.

They let me go in the hairdressing salon after the six months when they had promised to make me permanent. I stayed at home for two days while Daddy made enquiries. On the third night, he told me to report the next morning to the drapery shop in the village.

I was six months there behind a counter piled with patterns and balls of wool, when a letter came in my name calling me for interview to the new shirt factory below the village. He had never told me he had even applied. I was taken on with a hundred and twenty others.

The plant was brand new, everything so spick and span, and there were loads of girls just turned fifteen like myself. They let us play the radio all day as we sat at the machines and the older women came round with baskets to collect the finished garments. The Beatles were coming to Dublin and there was such excitement in work you couldn't imagine. Two of the girls had tickets and walked around like queens, while the rest of us arranged to meet up and stand outside the Adelphi to try and catch a glimpse of them.

There were thousands there, pushing and milling, and

then as the first show came out, the fighting began. The girls behind me started pulling my hair to get up nearer and the police charged down Abbey Street after the gangs of boys. I fell in the crush and cut my knee open. A policeman pushed the people back and lifted me out as I put my arms around his neck and clung to him in terror. They brought me home in a squad car, crammed with other girls who'd been hurt.

All the way home I prayed Daddy would be out, but he came to the door when the car pulled up. He looked so slight and feeble there with shame in his eyes as if the world was slipping away from him. He grabbed me by the hair in the garden and pulled me inside until he was pressed right up against me in the hallway. I could feel his breath as he raised his hand and I cowered, waiting for the slap to come down across my face. Instead, he just lowered it again and shook his head.

'I'll lock you in that room upstairs,' he said, 'till you learn not to disgrace me.' And he grabbed hold of my coat and pushed me ahead of him up the stairs. I was sobbing and tried to put my arms round him but he just shoved me on to the bed in this room and unscrewed the light bulb. He locked the door and left me sitting in the darkness. It was a Friday evening. From the window I could see the young people coming home from the pictures in groups, singing and enjoying the last drags of cigarettes before they reached their houses. And later on, the couples from the dances, on scooters or on foot, quiet now and anxious to avoid notice, standing against the dark leaves of the bushes fronting Mrs Finnegan's house with their arms around each other and only their mouths moving.

Johnny came in and I waited, hearing him ask where I was. I could hear their voices raised in argument, followed by the sitting-room door slamming. Then my father's feet came, one step, two step, like the old bogeyman. Was he coming to forgive me? Was he coming with his belt to beat me? The steps went into his bedroom and I heard the door close. There was complete silence in the house, yet I knew none of us were asleep. All night I kept waiting for Johnny to come. I'd say to myself, he's waiting for Daddy to cool down, in another ten minutes he'll climb the stairs. Or he's searching in the kitchen for the spare key, any minute now he'll come for me.

The darkness in the room was unbearable because I could not control it. I kept on imagining all kinds of things; my mother was sitting by the door in a chair, the furniture was swaying in the dark around me, floorboards were creaking on the landing. But nothing happened and nobody came, until finally towards dawn I fell asleep from exhaustion.

'I'll dream of them tonight,' said the small, fat fifteen-year-old girl whose eyes were shining and forehead damp as she tottered out into O'Connell Street like somebody possessed.

There was a tiny man with a red nose and spectacles standing on a wooden box outside the Evening Press *offices preaching about salvation. But he was talking to himself. Outside the cinema, a row of stout policemen with their arms linked were heaving strenuously against a frantic sea of young people. Girls were screaming inside. They screamed at the pictures in the programmes or if somebody shouted 'Beatles!' The atmosphere was hot and sharp: full of power and perfume and a frightening excitement.*

But when the curtain finally rose on THEM, the house erupted into one mad, thunderous noise, that continued right until the cries for more were drowned by the National Anthem.

This morning it was 'B'-Day plus one as the city began to clean up the debris from the Beatles invasion. Motorists made their way through the shambles of Abbey Street, while workers replaced the plate glass windows which fell victim to teenage hysteria.

Trouble began after the first of the two shows when more than two thousand people leaving the cinema 'mingled' with those going in. Members of the St John Ambulance Brigade attended to injured people on the spot while crowds ran riot around them.

Said a Garda sergeant whose cap was knocked off by a flying object, 'I have seen everything now. This is really mad. What can have got into them? You would imagine the country was in the middle of a revolution instead of welcoming four fugitives from a barber's shop.'

On the Saturday morning I knocked, but Johnny had gone away to town. I could hear Daddy in the room below silently pacing. I kept crying out for food and water until he finally appeared. He left the tea and sandwiches on the dresser and never once spoke. I wished to God he would scream at me or beat me black and blue, but he punished me instead with his silence.

I had had to pee in an old vase of my mother's that I was afraid to show him. By seven o'clock every muscle of my body was tense, my nails were bitten through, my head was drumming. I felt like the man in the paper who had been buried alive. I began to shriek like an animal and hurl myself against the door and that is where Johnny discovered me.

This is the bit the girl knows by heart. *Where Johnny discovered me*. These are the words she will say to herself in the long afternoons when the woman is working. Sitting in the chair watching over the bed where her nightdress is stretched on top of the sheets. She leans her head forward every time the story reaches here and gazes at the woman's lips.

Johnny came home at nine o'clock and when my father wouldn't give him the key, he went upstairs and kicked the door in. He found me lying in a pool of urine with blood crusted on my forehead. He carried me into the bathroom and locked the door, then filled the tub and sponged me down. I remember that his hands moved with a gentleness I had not thought him capable of. It was the first time he'd touched me in over two years.

He pulled a clean nightdress over my head and laid me back gently in my bed. Though I was groggy and only half-aware, I could feel a tremor in his hands as he drew the blankets over me and whispered, 'Don't worry, sis, I'll look after you. I'll never leave you alone with him again.'

Then he closed the door and marched down to confront my father standing defeated in the kitchen.

The girl lies back against the wall, her limbs stretched out, her breath coming quicker. But the woman stares at the floor as if by now only talking to herself.

That night he came again to my room, but more hesitant and shy than when we were young. He drew the blankets back slowly and waited to see if I would complain. His body was stronger than before, so that in the darkness he felt like a grown man. And I clung to him and allowed his hands to wander wherever they wanted to over me. His fingers found me and I sucked in my breath as he rubbed them back and forth.

I was nervous now and frightened but yet I didn't want him to stop even though I knew that it was wrong. My hands performed all the old tricks that he had taught me when I was ten. But I was fifteen now and knew there were no guardian angels to be excluded or wronged. He panted beside me so loudly I had to cover his mouth and then he lay flat like a dead weight against my side. And all he said was 'I'm sorry, sis,' over and over again.

The Casino cinema was taken over by the new supermarket and there was nothing left in the evening except the bus to town. Shoppers queuing at the meat counter could gaze up to the old balcony at trainee managers stacking cardboard boxes where suspicious ushers had once trained their torches.

Workmen began to fell the wood to build a dual carriageway that would slice the village in half. She watched the trees fall, every one of which seemed to contain a memory. A picnic of children sharing gur-cake and water, autumn afternoons with Johnny searching for conkers, the trunk her lover would have held her against. Blue tar was spilt and rolled into shape and, like a token replacement, tiny shoots of trees planted that the local youths smashed in disgust. Only the rivulet survived, swirling unnoticed through its narrow gorge.

The children of the estate were growing up and finding jobs or waiting at bus stops with two cases for the boat train. All the way to London, the train's wheels chanting *you'll never go back, you'll never go back*. New estates were springing up in the fields where she used to walk. Lorries loaded down with furniture moved along the finished side of the carriageway.

Two weeks after the Beatles came I arrived home to find Daddy in tears. There was no light on in the dining-room where he sat alone and I know that he had been there for hours, staring down at the wedding photograph in his hand as the features were gradually obliterated by the darkness. He turned to me in bafflement, and said, 'President

Kennedy has been shot. Has the whole world gone crazy or what?'

I wanted to put my hand out to him as he passed but I was no longer able to. He leaned heavily on the banisters when he went slowly to his room. After that, he rarely spoke to us, as if all his pride and hope was gone.

We had the house to ourselves and could do what we liked. Johnny and I bought a record-player between us and his friends called now to the sitting-room to play cards and listen to music. I'd come in with big pots of tea and toast for them and fall in love with each in turn, and they'd always shout down to me in the kitchen on their way out where I read romance magazines alone.

I had new friends in the shirt factory and we laughed and chatted to each other among the clattering machines. At lunch-time we'd sit out on the steps and wave back at the lads unloading the vans. Every Friday night, we'd gather at the bus stop to go to the pictures or dancing. I'd soak for half an hour in the bath and use the Lady Manhattan talc I'd splashed out five bob for.

The Friday evening bus to town. They occupy the back seat on top: eight of them squashed against the blue leather, five with beehive hairstyles, one looking like Priscilla Lane. Frames of evening sunlight flicker between the houses. One girl is laughing hysterically, inhaling noisy gulps of air as though she were choking. Whenever she falters, another begins and then another, each setting the other off, with the original joke long forgotten. The boys in the top seats cast slick glances back at them and shout down the aisle.

O'Connell Street is packed, the crowds crossing from side to side oblivious to the hooting lines of cars. Long snakes form outside the cinemas, a busker plays 'Love, Love Me Do'. Inside the darkness of the large picture palace they watch James Garner in his officer's uniform confronting Julie Andrews and Joyce Grenfell. The cinema echoes with shouts and catcalls, the usher's torch bobs across the rows. They agree it's not as good as *My Fair Lady* or *Goldfinger*.

The bouncers are unfriendly at the ballroom door, an off-duty Garda, uncomfortable in dicky-bow and suit, says, 'Will you sleep with me tonight?' and grins, trying to squeeze them as he allows each girl in. They sip lemonade on the balcony and watch the band below imitate the English hit parade note for note. The floor below fills up, one by one they are asked to dance.

She dances with four or maybe five boys, their conversation always the same. In the embarrassed silence after each set she mumbles her thanks and backs away, wandering off to find a girlfriend and stand together surveying the floor. They try not to show their excitement as they whisper confidences in each other's ears. Towards the end of the night they're part of the crush around the stage, the lead singer's hand reaching down to theirs as he sings *Ave Maria*.

They gather forces when the lights come on, wait for two of their friends to finish kissing the boys they've met, and then begin the long walk home where a girl begins to laugh hysterically, inhaling noisy gulps of air down her throat as her friends join in.

I had always thought of him waiting at the lamp-post opposite the house, gazing sadly up towards my window. Often I tried to imagine that it was him in the darkness when Johnny switched the light out. Everywhere I went in the house his eyes seemed to follow as though he were haunting me. And Daddy never said a word, about what hour we came in or what we did. He sat in the kitchen or went to bed with the radio, his only companion. Johnny would be there when I came in, listless after a night of disappointment in town.

'Come on in, sis, just for a while. Nobody will know,' he'd say, and try to take my hands in his. 'Please sis, I need you,' and though I'd struggle and try to push him away, we both knew that it would always end with the pair of us sprawled on the sitting-room floor.

When we lay there, it seemed that nothing had changed, as if somehow we had turned back the clock and were children once again. His voice was the only constant in my world, lulling me as he whispered, 'We're free of him, sis, we only need each other,' and I'd give way, desperate for the pleasure he offered.

Then, on the stairs afterwards, I'd feel a stab of fear passing my father's room with my clothes bundled up against my bare flesh. It was as if I was deliberately sinning against him, against all the years when he had dominated my every thought and action, against the guilt I had felt when I upset or appeared to shame him.

Johnny seemed to be right that we were free, there was no longer anything to believe in, and yet the secret gnawed like a cancer inside me. I knew that it was wrong. I knew that it was dangerous and we could never step out into the future until it was finished. Even before the pleasure was fully over from his fingers I could feel the sense of let-down, of shame, and I knew that Johnny could feel it too, his ears alert for any noise, his eagerness to be up which he tried to hide.

And every time I always said that it must end, and so it would until the next weekend night when I saw the light beckoning in the sitting-room window as the girls left me on the corner.

johnny johnny lover boy, will come out when we're alone, when the castle door is shut, and the wicked witch is gone. come to play, come to shout, turn the bedroom inside out. bring the world in for me, whispering our secret story. johnny johnny waiting there, past the bogeyman on the stair. johnny johnny has to hide, before he comes to claim his bride.

One Friday night we went to see the Capitol Showband, I danced with a boy with hair below his collar. 'What's your name?' I asked, and when he replied 'Daithi Lacha' we both just stood there on the floor and laughed. *Daithi*

Lacha, David Mouse. He lived up the west and asked to walk me home. The girls giggled when I told them I'd see them in work on Monday.

It was the middle of summer, we could have walked for miles. He took my hand and I hoped he'd never let it go as we talked about everything that entered our heads. At the corner of my street, he lowered his head cautiously and I lifted my face to meet him. I could feel the soft leaves against my hair as I leaned back into the shadows and pressed my hand over his which hovered lightly on my breast. We promised to meet on the Wednesday night and he stood there watching me from the corner until I went in.

Music was coming from the sitting-room and as the door handle turned, I felt like an animal in a trap. I only wanted to get away. I was exhilarated and strong. To be touched by someone else would seem like a desecration.

'Johnny, I'm going to bed,' I whispered, as he crept into the hall. He put a finger to his lips and began to draw me in. He was more nervous than usual, I think he had been drinking. I couldn't resist him as he pulled my wrists, I just kept repeating, 'Don't, Johnny,' again and again. Every touch seemed to be destroying the memory of the boy. I could feel tears on my cheeks when he persisted and I lay there, stiff and unresisting.

Johnny grew angry then and must have raised his voice. The record had spun to a close and Daddy was standing at the door in his dressing-gown. My skirt was up above my waist and Johnny was stretched on top of me.

'Get up,' he shouted at Johnny, 'you've taken my home away from me, but you won't take my daughter.'

Johnny stood up and stepped back against the wall. He said nothing, his eyes fixed on the door. I scrambled up to try and run out but Daddy pushed me back.

'Right, come on then, you young buck, let's see if you can fight men as easily.'

Daddy's face was red and he was trembling. I could see that Johnny didn't want to fight. He kept backing away as Daddy circled him. Then he put his guard down, lowered his head and simply took the punches as they swung at him. What I remember most was the silence in the room, me in one corner crying quietly, Johnny with his head bowed and blood running down his face, and only the sound of Daddy's breath and his hand thudding against flesh as the sweat rolled over his forehead.

It seemed to last an eternity until Daddy stopped, all the anger drained from his body and his face looking the way it had when he came down the stairs eight years before to say that Mammy was dead. He turned and walked slowly back up to his room. We heard the door slam and still Johnny didn't raise his head. I stood in the corner and it felt like a thousand miles lay between us. Then he said, 'I'm sorry, sis, I'm sorry,' and walked past me into the kitchen.

I followed him to where he held his face under the cold tap in the huge white sink and tried to help him as he had once helped me, but he shrugged away from my touch when I put my fingers to his forehead and said in that quiet voice, 'Just go to bed, sis, please.'

When I came down the next morning he was gone. The old suitcase that used to be under the stairs was missing and none of his clothes were in the hotpress. In a drawer in the kitchen I had a cake hidden with eighteen candles. It would have been his birthday that Sunday.

'She must be in love,' they say, noticing her silence in the factory. 'Eh, Sandra, is it Daithi Lacha from the west? Did you give him a nibble of your cheese?' they shout across the loud machines and she smiles back and says nothing. She often thinks of how he must have stood that Wednesday at the corner of Parnell Street, his hope evaporating as the last person climbed from each bus. Yet thoughts of him always lead her back to the image of Johnny's bleeding face held beneath the tap, and the isolation she is now trapped within.

Infinite afternoons when Radio Caroline blares out the Rolling Stones and the Marvelettes, and naked electric light strains her eyes as she sits, carefully stitching at her machine while the factory echoes with shouts and laughter. Her friends, imagining a failed lover, grow protective and cluster around her. On her way home she pauses by the rivulet which glints like a silver needle stitching together her life. The sting of a single nettle in an overhung glade whose poison darkened both their blood.

For over a year and a half her father accepts each meal

in silence and never speaks unless to request something. She washes dishes in the small kitchen while he stares through the window at the garden becoming overgrown since the spring before when he last touched it. One evening she walks through the bare remains of the wood to the fields where the new estates are being built. Children run through the open buildings, dodging the old watchman in the corrugated iron hut.

In the hallway on her return she hears the radio, *Ceili House* echoing from the dining-room. She opens the door to bring in his tea and finds him sprawled out beside his chair. His pipe had burnt a small hole in the rug that his eyes appear to be staring at in disbelief. A white smear had dribbled from his lips and the newspaper covers half the floor.

She makes the phone call from a neighbour's house who returns to the sitting-room with her. She kneels beside him when his mouth tries to form words, but all she can catch is a faint choking in his throat. She takes his hand in the ambulance, feeling the sides sway as they zig-zag through the traffic, and after an hour sitting in the corridor a doctor confirms that he's suffered a stroke.

That night is the first she ever spends alone in the house. She leaves the light on in her bedroom and tries to pray, but all she can hear are the tiny creaks and tappings of the beams settling like clay around her.

The hardest thing to watch was his helplessness. In my childhood he had overshadowed everything so that my whole life was centred around pleasing him. But now he could do nothing for himself. Every evening I would visit the hospital and he'd lie there trying to speak. One side of him was paralysed and the lip hung down without support. From the other side of his mouth he could mumble words, though after he had spoken them, the horror in his eyes showed you they were not the ones he meant. His tongue would curl up trying to explain and then lapse into baffled silence.

I'd bring him shirts he couldn't wear and books he couldn't hold and sit at the end of the bed feeling foolish as I gibbered away to fill that silence. I'd watch the nurse trying to feed him, patient and always good-humoured. His mouth would clap shut before the spoon reached it and the bite would be scattered all over his chin.

'Now, just relax and open your mouth,' she'd say, and I'd watch the lips press tightly shut.

'Now close it,' she'd say, and thrust the spoon between the lips when they opened while his eyes registered amazement. I could feel those eyes never leaving me, even when the nurse had been round for a fifth time and all the families had departed. As I kissed him and walked towards the door, I could sense his head trying to turn and follow me as if terrified at being abandoned.

On the last night I saw him, he seemed to have recovered. He managed a smile when I sat on the bed. Behind us, the nurses had drawn the curtains around a man who was moaning in pain. I remember how spring was trying to break through. Fresh flowers stood in the vase beside his locker and the light was soft when it came through the window. There was power in his fingers as he gripped my hand and during the whole hour, we never once spoke.

We just stared at each other like we shared a secret and after a time I realized both our eyes were filled with tears. It was as if the pair of us were learning how to forgive without needing to understand. When I was going, he wouldn't release my hand until I took the little silver miraculous medal I wore around my neck and pressed it down into his palm instead. As I kissed him goodbye, I put my arms around his neck for the first time since I was a child.

That evening I walked home from town, up Gardiner Street where old ladies were leaning out of windows, and followed the railway tracks along by the canal past the high walls of Mountjoy jail. I felt a lightness I hadn't known for months as I made plans about how I would fix the house for his return.

It was one o'clock when the policeman woke me from my sleep and the squad car took me back into town. I kept thinking this was a dream, I'd wake up and it would be morning again. Four nurses knelt around the bed, being led through the decades of the rosary. A nun in white robes whispered to me.

'He had a second massive stroke. It happened so suddenly we couldn't prise the medal out of his hands.'

★　　★　　★

Only the altar is lit in the dark church. She kneels in the pew nearest the locked gates of the alcove where the coffin rests. The ivory limbs of the crucified figure hang in shadow now. Mass-cards and wreaths from neighbours and workmates line the coffin. She knows, for his sake, she must be strong till it is over. In the morning it rains. She travels in the black car alone with Mrs Whelan and an uncle who had come from London. A handful of friends from Rutland Street and some neighbours shelter under umbrellas. The priest intones in Latin, the gravediggers lower the coffin slowly with ropes.

Standing back among the tombstones without a hat in the rain, she sees Johnny alone, hesitant to approach. He comes back to the house and helps to dispense sandwiches. The uncle leaves for the boat; individually the neighbours file out until there is only the pair of them on each side of the fire listening to the April rain blown against the house.

'I was afraid to come back,' he says, 'afraid of what I can't control.' She doesn't reply and, for the first time since the funeral, begins to cry.

'Stay, Johnny, don't leave me tonight. I couldn't bear it alone.'

The words are committed to the darkened house and it is she who leads him up those high stairs, as though grief were a pain that some greater anguish might eclipse.

'Anything,' is all she says, 'do anything,' and when he penetrates her for the first time ever, all she can think of is the clay capsizing as she feels each sharp thrust. Pressing down on her in the darkness he is stranger, brother, father, lover, all coming together in this single agonizing act. His lips drown in her hair again as he cries out in a muffled gasp, but this time she knows instinctively that she will never see him again. Yet over and over in the darkness she gives her body to him as though cutting loose all the barriers of grief in a final desperate gesture of loyalty.

Later, when she hears the bed springs creak, she holds her eyelids closed over the film of tears and pretends, for his sake, to be asleep as she lies among the tumbled blankets with the streaks of blood dried into her thighs and listens to him furtively dressing to leave. Just this once she wishes him to be strong as if it would somehow justify her sacrifice. She listens and is disappointed when he pauses uncertainly at the bedroom door, a timid, hesitant young man stripped of all childhood bravado.

The days that followed are all blurred together. I was allowed time off work and couldn't bear to be alone in the house. At one o'clock each night I had to get out, it seemed as if every room was freezing. I'd walk the streets for an hour or two and when I'd come home, the atmosphere was gone. Often in the evenings I would forget and lay out the table for two. I've his suits of clothes in that wardrobe still. I've never had the courage to throw them out. One night I dreamt I found his leg beneath the bed and I was carrying it in a box around the cemetery trying to find his grave.

The Corporation confirmed that I would still have the

house and I forced myself to try and think of other things. Some evenings I'd go out as far as Broom Bridge and walk back along the canal towards town. It had become the coldest spring for decades. Although there was sunshine by day, each night a heavy frost gripped everything, so that long stretches of the water were frozen over.

Gangs of children smashed the ice and threw it across the stiff surface. I bent down on the bank and broke a piece off. It skidded towards the far bank with a shrill, tinkling sound, sliding away into a hundred pieces. It was a lovely sensation, like the past breaking up. I broke piece after piece off, not caring if anybody looked. Lovers stood against the huge wooden locks where the water beneath the ice sprayed out in wild thundering foam.

I felt like a patient convalescing, gathering strength to begin my real life. I was nineteen years of age and had never been outside my native city. The Friday after I went back to work, the Dixielanders were playing in town. I joined the girls once again at the bus stop.

When I missed the first one I tried to put it down to grief. The shock was too much for my body. Always it had been at the back of my mind, but I couldn't believe it would happen just from that one night. Every morning for the week before I was due again I'd be standing outside the church in the dark at twenty-past seven with a handful of pensioners. After Mass, I'd hurry to work not daring to think of the future.

One morning the sickness came over me as I was coming

out the church door. It was as though fate was laughing at me. I had to run to the wall at the back of the car-park and endure the stares of the rest of the congregation. It didn't come the second time and I panicked. I searched Drumcondra for Johnny's digs and could find only a forwarding address for Manchester.

That night I crushed up forty aspirins in a bottle of lemonade. I went out walking in the street, hoping to be discovered collapsed in a doorway. I don't think I was right in my head. I felt that the neighbours were watching me, they didn't approve that I lived here alone. They had always done my father down, but I would not disgrace him. I put two fingers down my throat and spewed up the tablets. I would not give way to anyone. This was my home and my Daddy's before me. I went straight to work to earn money to keep it, having watched the sun rise over the cold industrial estate.

She wears a small black star on her overcoat and always the same loose dresses. They put her silence down to delayed shock and mourning, in the canteen of the factory. On Friday evenings the girls ask her out, but she always smiles and refuses now. Sometimes they see her, walking around the streets near her home. One says she often stands on the bridge over the Tolka, oblivious to the people or the traffic around her. Later on, she never removes her thick coat even though she is sweating at the machine. Experienced eyes watch her walk in and out of the toilet.

'She's pregnant, and that's a fact,' they say, 'and that fellow she was going out with must have left her.'

She shifts uneasily when they approach her after work and runs without speaking out of the gate. She pushes past the neighbours with her eyes kept down, and keeps the door locked and the curtains pulled. When Mrs Whelan and the others call, she only shouts at them from behind the closed door.

You were like some kind of strange invader. You were just there, beating within me all the time. When I was by myself I would talk to you inside, just like I am talking to you now. Two letters went to Johnny and the second was returned, marked *not known at this address*.

All I could think of was the house being taken away from me. I sensed my father still trapped here, as if his ghost was burdened by this new disgrace. And I knew I could not fail him now, the way that I had failed him in life. All the time I kept thinking, something must happen, it just can't go on like this. At the same time every month I returned to pray in that church. The funeral had cost almost all my father's savings. I hadn't a penny to my name, and I knew that my job was gone from me the moment I confessed.

At night I would imagine that Johnny was about to board the boat from Liverpool. *He'll be here at dawn in a taxi*, I'd whisper to you in my mind to help me sleep. He was strong and defiant. He would take us away from here. Every morning I'd watch from this window as the postman on his bicycle passed the house. By December I was huge and overdue.

He's bound to come for Christmas, I told you, and placed a burning candle in every window on Christmas Eve. All night I waited alone in the sitting-room, watching the bobbing yellow flame flicker on the sill.

The waters broke at two o'clock and she staggered from one bedroom to the other. The pains came closer and closer together as she boiled water in the kitchen. She carried the saucepan up to her old bedroom, spilling most of the boiling water on the floor. When the child came, she seemed black as if touched with the mark of the devil. As she cut the cord and pulled her up still covered with the slime of birth to hold her in her arms, she cried and felt the pain would never end. The afterbirth came like a pulverized misshapen twin on the cold squares of lino. She washed the tiny girl carefully, pausing to check if she had stopped breathing. One moment she held her like a prize and the next she wanted to kill her. The little fists were clenched up towards the eyes, as if the child was protecting herself.

Before dawn came, she suddenly longed to be rid of her. The child lay on the bedspread, sickly looking and never crying as though it were about to die. She couldn't bear to look at it, like a ghost that had crawled from her stomach to haunt her. The woman's nails bit into her own skin. Still crying, she searched in the attic for old newspapers, and carefully wrapped the infant she feared in them.

A small room, lit only by the streetlight shafting through the ripped curtain. Two women, one huddled beneath the window without moving, the other seated in a chair constantly talking. Between them, the light slides across the dirty lino. Every story the girl knows by heart. They are the faces who populate the room. She sleeps with her eyes open and dreams. The park is a vast expanse of concrete filled with trees the colour of wallpaper. A boy and girl run forward from their parents towards the river that stretches into the horizon. The parents turn to watch them. All four have the face of her mother, the heads too large for the small frames of the children's bodies.

As they throw white flakes of paper into the water the red worm slithers out on to the bank, her hero, the only colour in the dream, fleshy muscles contracting as it slithers towards her, brushing through the people in the park, coiling between the grey headstones and onward through cavities and partitions along the row of houses, its blind mouth chewing life out of life, the red flesh contracting as it crawls to claim her. She wakes, unnoticed, and hears the voice continue.

It was after four o'clock and the streets were empty. I stepped over the wall so as not to squeak the gate and went down the road in the shadow of the hedges. There was nothing I could feel any more. My legs were unsteady, my body hurt. You never cried or stirred and I hoped that you were already dead. I was just so scared, I didn't know what to do. They'd put me out of the house, I knew they would. They'd drive me from this street and from my job. I had nobody that I could trust. I was just too frightened to bring you into the world.

I climbed down the steps beside the green and waited in the shadows by the pile of rocks till a car went by. Across the road I could see a light still on in a bedroom of the parish priest's house set back in the garden with the old trees and tall grass which always looked so inviting. I ran past and when I came to the side of the church I grew terrified. I stood as though expecting Christ himself to come out from that granite wall and confront me.

It must have been fifteen minutes that I waited there, holding you wrapped in those old papers and then I heard footsteps, like an old man's, from the roadway and I started forward to leave you on the step of the side porch and ran off up the main street of the village, past the post office and the pubs. I hid in an alley-way for a few moments to see if anyone was following me and then, when old Turlough passed, I raced back down the hill on to the side of the new carriageway and slipped down into the gully by the stream.

I could hear the twigs breaking as I rolled down the bank and feel them snapping into my flesh when my skirt rode up. I came to rest against the base of one of the old trees and could see the stream murmuring just a few feet from my head. There was no sound anywhere, nobody would see if I just kept rolling. It was such bliss to imagine myself lying face up in one of the rocky pools to be found in the morning by the schoolchildren playing there. And you know, I could see it so vividly that it wasn't me floating on the water. It was somebody else who had all my sins and my flaws and I was watching up above her, free for the first time, no longer feeling any grief or pain but just a sheer, soothing numbness.

And then, as though the very grass and the gnarled trunk were speaking to me, I knew that I could simply not give in. It was as if the swirling water and the clay there had a spirit of their own that was giving me back my strength. I realized that all those sins were not sins, that Christ hadn't come forth from the wall, that the only sin was the sin of abandoning you dead or alive, in that old newspaper on the step of the church. And I knew that I loved you because you were the only thing left to me in the world. I knew that I would never abandon you as I had been abandoned, that you would never go through the ordeals that had been mine. You're all I have, child. You're all I've ever cared for.

The blare of loudspeakers in the summer evening. The host is carried past by the priests in full dress. Young men of the FCA march behind with empty rifles in a guard of honour. And behind them the Scouts and the Cubs, the

Guides and the Little Flowers of Mary in white dresses. And then the schoolchildren, class by class with the parents behind.

Each house is decked with bunting and a tricolour hangs from a neighbour's window. Pictures of the Sacred Heart watch from behind scrubbed panes as people stand at the gates to give back the responses to the prayers the priest intones into the loudspeaker.

One house has no bunting, no picture. The curtains are pulled shut. The baby's lips stop suckling and slowly the girl prises them from her nipple. Her blouse still open, she cuddles the child to her skin in the curtained twilight. The metallic voice from outside fills the room, like the voices of the German soldiers surrounding the castle in the film Johnny had once taken her to see in the Casino. She shivers and moves her fingers gently to cover the baby's mouth.

This was not the way I meant it to happen, you know, but who could I turn to? I dragged myself to work for the first week, feeling that every eye in the place was watching me, that every person knew. I would run up the street praying you were not crying and I could see the neighbours standing in their doorways. One evening Mrs Whelan said, 'Are you sure you're all right, Sandra, is anything the matter?' I almost pushed her off the pavement and ran inside.

I wrote to Johnny in England, care of the factory where

somebody said their brother had seen him working. I told him the whole story. I kept thinking I don't need to tell them, Johnny will be here soon and he'll take us away. We'll live somewhere in England as man and wife. Oh, I was so stupid. It was like thinking that Mammy would come back from the grave.

At the end of the week, I stopped working for fear you would be found. I cancelled the milk and the bread and answered the door to nobody. I lived on white bread and tea to conserve money to buy the things you needed, and I'd walk to town to get them for fear of being seen purchasing them locally.

I slept holding you in my arms, afraid to move in case I would crush you, and whenever I blacked out into sleep, I would have the same dream. Officials hammering on the door searching for you, with the neighbours watching from their gardens, saying 'This is a respectable street, we don't want her sort living here.' And Sister Carmel coming up the stairs in her black hood to carry you away to the orphanage.

You were a few weeks old now and I imagined the police coming, being taken away in a squad car for not reporting your birth. The endless questioning in the cold room and two English policemen calling one morning to Johnny's digs to arrest him. My mother's face seemed to hover sadly above the bed saying, 'You're holding me back with your pain. I will never get to Heaven unless you let go.'

Then one night you cried for hours even though I almost smothered you with a pillow to try and drown it. I was starving with the hunger and felt suicidal. You had a fever and were shaking and finally I ran out through the streets to hammer on Mrs Whelan's door. The trucks from Meath swept past, catching me in their headlights. She came down in her nightdress and opened the door a fraction to look at me standing on the path staring wildly at her. I wanted to tell her. I knew that I couldn't carry on alone. But I didn't know how to say the words. I was an outcast and knew that I would be held to blame.

'What's wrong, Sandra?' she said, and I just turned around and ran away from her, ignoring her voice as she called after me. I kept circling the block, afraid to go back and see you dead. I finally stopped outside the house and listened. There was no sound from within and I was sure that you had died. I climbed up the stairs slowly, I don't know what I expected to find. All I could think of was Daddy's spade in the shed and would I be strong enough to use it?

You were sleeping peacefully with all trace of your fever gone. I climbed in beside you and for the first time since you were born I allowed myself to cry, on and on silently till the pillowcase was saturated by the time dawn broke along the grey street outside.

Sir,

Further to our letter of last month, we wish to repeat to you that we believe Sandra O'Connor to have given birth to a child in her own home. We have heard the child crying from outside on a number of occasions and as neighbours, we have tried to approach Sandra several times. She doesn't appear to work any more and refuses to open the door to anyone. The curtains in her house are closed at all times and as we have not heard the child crying now for several weeks, we are most anxious for its safety. As far as we can understand, you have taken no action in response to our two previous letters. Let us remind you that this is a Corporation house and that you do have responsibilities for what happens within it.

Yours sincerely,
Joseph & Maire Flaherty.

Eventually I had to find a new job, of course. There was no money left and I used to walk into town and steal cans of baby food from the big stores, until one day I was caught by a guard in a uniform. I bit into his hand till the blood ran and when he let go, I dashed through the crowd of people and he lost me in the street.

You were such a quiet child. It seemed as if you knew that your life had to be a secret between us. I put you down on the floor and you learnt to crawl and to laugh and clap your hands when I made funny faces. And then one day you said *Mammy* and were so delighted with yourself that you repeated the word over and over for hours. It was the only word you ever spoke and after a time you even stopped saying that. I would spend hours bending over you saying baby words and funny talk and you would only stare back at me with big bewildered eyes and then look past as if there was somebody else in the room. The smell was what I hated most in those days. The rows and rows of nappies I was unable to hang outside, always dripping from the rail in the kitchen, their scent filling up the house.

A new factory opened and I was taken on. I stayed up with you the whole night before I began, playing and laughing so you would be asleep for the time I was away. And then I came home exhausted after the first day and sat up with you again till dawn that night and every other until I discovered that you didn't mind being left on your own. You sat there on the floor ignoring the few toys I put around you and stared off into space as I put on my coat and warned you to stay quiet. And in the evening when I came home you'd be sitting there almost as though you hadn't moved since the time I left. And you know, you've never changed, you've just grown.

You're a woman now and you still sit there day after day without speaking. I know you can speak! I know! I've heard noises when I've stood outside, Stony Bother, Scrubby Meadow, Shallon, names of nowhere, things I didn't teach you. You cried and you once said *Mammy*, therefore you have a voice which you won't use and you won't use it so as just to torment me, just to keep me alone and out of your world. It's spite! It's your way of getting back at me. I know! Speak to me! Speak to me, you little bitch! I've given up my life for you! How could I let you out now, how could you live without me? Bitch! I'm going to shake you until you speak, I'm going to pinch you and beat you. Stop staring at me! I'm coming for you now! Don't think you can get away. I'll make you talk yet!

johnny johnny sing for me, make the coat-hangers play: shake the plates around the house and make mammy go away. johnny johnny is my friend, he will come out to sing, when mammy goes off to work and thinks she has locked me in. johnny johnny can't feel you, just this tearing, tearing pain: throw open the doors of the press, make the room glow again. can feel her hands crashing off my skull, come out johnny johnny and prove your love. slam that door which shouldn't be ajar, i dread the light coming from the stairs. want to be alone with you in the dark, where johnny johnny we could talk and talk. she dragging my hair into a knot, don't keep your place or i'll be caught. knock over the wardrobe, shake the grate: save me johnny johnny before it is too late.

My God, I never meant to hurt you. I often wonder how you're still breathing at times. I'll stop now, look I won't touch you. I'll never hit you again. Can't you see you make me angry? Why don't you reach out to me? Sometimes, we're like strangers. Here, I'll help you into bed and fix the blankets for you. No? Well stay there so.

You know, it's strange how those first days when I

did nothing stretched into years. I always thought that something would happen. It couldn't just go on, world without end, forever. But Johnny never returned for us, and we merely grew here, inward and stupid, watching each night turn into morning, like a string of hard beads I kept running blindly through my fingers.

At night, after we'd sat up in this room and I'd played with you until you'd fallen asleep, I'd lie awake in my parents' bed and juggle those three choices over and over in my mind. What could I do? You're not normal, you're not right in the head. I don't know the word – autistic, retarded? But there's something wrong. How could I bring you out of this house? I'd be sent to jail, Johnny would be in jail, and you would be locked away in some hospital.

My Daddy always told me when I was a little girl never to go beyond the corner of the street. The last house had an ornate wooden porch with crazy paving and ivy growing on its walls. I knew so little then I thought a Chinaman lived there. Never talk to strangers, he would say, never venture out into the world. In this street we can hold our head up, no more tenements, no more poverty. No more Rutland Street. No more sharing a toilet with three families. Never let the world see grief or fear or emotion.

He built a house for himself, of silence and frigidity, he encased it in these walls where we are living still. I often think he dwells here yet, imposing his will upon us. I never knew enough to look after you, child, I've never had any friends in this new factory. Every remark and joke of theirs

I've told you has been made up in my own head. I've always been too frightened to talk to people, afraid that in any intimacy I'd let the mask slip. This house and you are all I possess, and when I walk out that front door my whole life stops.

Over the back wall they came, across the littered waste ground. Their feet sunk noiselessly in the long wild grass of the garden when they dropped. One youth fell forward and his hands plunged into the savage nettles, stiff as bamboo. They moved with difficulty through the debris and reached the darkened house.

'It looks fucking abandoned,' one said, and tried the heavily bolted back door. He climbed on to the window-ledge and banged the small frame till the latch sprang up. Reaching his hand in, he pulled the stiff handle of the bigger window, where the paint had peeled away with age. The warped frame opened slowly with a loud creak and as he stepped on to the inner sill, the woman appeared.

'This is my house!' she screamed, 'Get out! Get out!' His boot caught her beneath the throat and she fell back. His friend jumped in behind him and grabbed her hair. He twisted it in his hand saying, 'Where do you keep your money, you old wagon? Come on, you fucking battleaxe, or I'll cut your gee out!'

She screamed, and they hit her hard across the face. She felt a tooth loosen in her mouth and bit into the hand as it swung towards her again. The youth screamed and tried to jerk it away but she clung on like a ferret, her body pulled up from the floor as he retreated from her. His friend kicked her hard in the rib cage and she lost her grip and fell backwards on to the floor again.

'I'm going to screw the fucking arse off you,' the youth said, smashing the knick-knacks that had littered the mantelpiece for two decades on to the floor with his bloodsmeared hand. The woman said nothing and just pressed herself against the door of the room.

'Jesus, this house gives me the creeps. I don't think we'll find much bread here,' his friend said, and the youth held his injured hand to his lips and replied: 'These oul biddies would die sooner than use a bank. They always have a hundred or two for masses for their shagging souls stashed away under the floorboards or the mattress. Don't worry, we'll get it out of her!'

What struck her were their outside accents and the clothes, how they were the sort of people her father had always taught her to look up to. She pressed back harder against the door. They approached her carefully and one grabbed her by the hair and pulled her to him while the other reached down, ripping her skirt open as he tried to control the wildly kicking legs. He fell forward on to them and finally got them tightly together and against his chest. He lifted her up and his friend kept her in a headlock with her arm twisted behind her back as they carried her up the stairs.

At the top of the stairs, the youth paused for a moment

and then kicked open the door of the bedroom. He let the woman's feet drop and his friend hit her again as she fell so that she lay bleeding and unconscious on the floor. The youth ripped the curtain open so that the streetlight caught the sweat trickling down his face. In the press behind him, the coat-hangers slowly began to swing and clash against each other. The window frame seemed to vibrate before his eyes and the bed beside him rattled back and forth. He turned and stared at the bed. Slowly, the girl rose on one elbow between the blankets, her lank hair falling away to reveal her face in the streetlight.

Both youths stood and began to shiver as they watched her rise. Then his friend screamed and ran down the stairs where the pictures were shaking on the wall. Gradually, the long fingers of the girl reached out and touched his hand.

'Johnny, Johnny,' her thin, childlike voice said. He felt the urine, hot and sticky, trickling down his thigh as he backed away and stumbled over the woman's body. Running down the stairs, it seemed to him that he was moving through mercury, so slowly did his limbs appear to function. He felt fingers, bony and small, pinch his back when he reached the hall, and swung his fist through the pane of glass in the door as though trying to waken himself from a nightmare. The glass shattered along the doorstep, moonlight latching on to it to ignite a thousand stars, as he raced, shivering, after his friend.

★   ★   ★

Somebody was always bound to come in the end. That was all I was certain of. For eighteen years I've waited here, guarding you and me, always knowing it was going to happen. My ribs hurt, I think one of them is broken. That's the first person since Johnny to touch my body. A conductor helping me on to a bus, a drunk stumbling against me in a crowd, the supermarket cashier pressing change into my hand – they're the only human touches except that night you warmed my hand, which I've known these eighteen years.

But it's over now, I tell you, it's over, daughter. How are we going to recognize our Saviour when he comes, how can we know what form he will take? Eighteen years I've waited for help, not knowing how to act. Every morning of it I've entered this room and paused for a moment with three choices before me as clear as dawn. Three rolls of a dice to decide our lives that I've always kept firmly clenched in my palm.

To lock you in here for yet another day to lie for ten hours with your vacant stare, while I sit at the endless orange peel of a conveyor belt, and worry that somebody will find you. To finish it now like I've often dreamt of, gently with a pillow or in one of those fits where I can't think straight, my hands shaking with my knuckles turning white clasped over the poker. And then hurry through the streets in terror of footsteps before somebody finds your body gummed to the mattress with blood. I would be free of responsibility at last, no matter what they did to me.

Or else in the starkness of dawn realize that we could

walk down those stairs with your hand in mine. Can you hear the sound of the milkmen going to work, heading down to the dairy by the carriageway? It will be another hour before the people start rising for buses. Below our window there's a rivulet. Johnny and I always wanted to follow it to the sea. It's been years since I stood beside it. They've cleared away the brambles and trees and piped most of it underground. But it's still running there and we could follow it yet, through the valley enclosed by the convent, through the gardens and down past the factories in Drumcondra.

I don't know where it leads to from there, I only know there must be a strand where sea birds would rise up like an explosion before us. We could be there before the people stirred, moving away from the nightmare of this room. Just the pair of us, standing with our backs to the land, fingers joined like schoolgirls taking some boy's hand and swallowing their pride. No bogeyman guards those stairs, only our fear keeps us trapped in this house. If I had the courage to lead you down, would you hold back, my daughter, or would you take my hand?

There is a city of the dead standing sentinel beyond her window. Through the gully, a rivulet frothing over rocks swirls down between them. Early light grains out the slabs of granite flecked with mud from tractor wheels. The living world seems to end beyond its walls and railings, yet even here life stirs invisibly downward. Beneath plastic wreaths and fonts it creaks forward incessantly. Death is only when growth stands still. To pass into light, to burn on in slow decay, to open to change is to be born again.

johnny johnny all gone and dead, now only cold air and light instead. never been this alone before, since johnny's angel came through the door. johnny's angel touched my hand, then johnny's angel screamed and ran. johnny's angel's hair was black, johnny's angel wore no mask: mammy's face broken in blood, now johnny's angel came for her. no voice left now to answer mine, no way to know if she is lying. mammy's approaching, arms outstretched, raise up my hands to protect my neck: so terrified to leave this world, cold and white outside if i uncurl.

When dawn had broken on the following morning, certain of the women gathered beyond the gates of the house. Like a stone that had been rolled back, the front door hung open. A young teenage boy gazed from beside his grandmother at tiny shards of glass glittering on the doorstep. Thirty-year-old lino, worn and threadbare, ran down the hall. Some could remember standing on it the day a young girl ran home from school. Some remembered a coffin being carried down the stairs. And the shadow of a broken man watching from behind lace as his daughter laughed and raced after her brother in the street. They shouted her name over and over, gazed in disbelief at old Mrs Whelan who had brought them here. The old man at the back of the crowd leaned on his stick to watch.

'Give me your shoulder's Johnny,' she said as, leaning heavily on her grandson and not knowing what to expect, Mrs Whelan led them painfully and cautiously up the path and into the hallway that stood as silent as a deserted churchyard in the early spring sunlight.

PART TWO

Victoriana

This is how I would sketch a self-portrait: barely enough light to discern the features of a figure stooped at the edge of the bed, the white bars of a cot outlined in the dimness, as still and grey as those new photographs. The child is so small as to be no more than a single brush stroke, a curve of blanket in the background, and yet her very smallness makes me, the figure, seem small too. I am so aware at this moment, as I listen to her last reluctant cry fading into a pattern of sleep, that I suddenly know that I am just one moment in history, one of an infinite line of fathers who watched at evening's end their children drift to sleep. They stretch behind me and before me, I as much a speck in their minds as they are in mine. And I feel so dwarfed by time, so insignificant and yet unique, taking my place here before the light goes, before I rise, closing the loft door softly, and descend to where my young wife lifts her head in the candlelight, smiles and looks back at the sewing in her lap.

A brown dog nestles near the fire, bothered by the heat but too lazy to move. He stretches on his stomach as though his limbs were amputated, lifts his head sideways to observe me and waits. I neither move nor speak but he knows it's his time. He rises, shakes himself and pads towards the door. I lift the latch and stare out. The wooded fields behind the cottages are quiet tonight, a few lights flickering from the farmhouse across from the barracks. The last tram waits to return to the city, the horses' breath discernible in the jets of gaslight at the convent entrance.

I look back at my wife, my daughter, my home. The few pieces of furniture we've gathered together, the gift of a mirror hung in a corner. And I'm suddenly scared for a reason I cannot comprehend. The dog brushes past me and looks back, the trees creak in the wind. I close the door and step outside, knowing the path I will take, the other me that I will become – younger, with an obsessive hunger. A carriage jangles on its ascent of Washerwoman's Hill. I avoid the route it will take, the road which swoops down through hawthorn bushes to the bridge. I take to the fields instead with an echo of that same illicit thrill. My wife and child retreat. For twenty minutes or more I will forget them, forget the present, the comfort of knowing a home. It's that old craving, diluted but still not cured, sending me stalking the woods by the back of Bridget's father's cottage down to where the streams meet, to the wall of the asylum which is the only home left to Bridget now. I want to forget as much as I need to remember, I'm torn between worlds like a hare caught by hounds. But I'll stand under those oaks by the stream's edge, just beyond the sphere of light from the gatekeeper's lodge, and remember her voice, her eyes as they stared about the walls of her room, remember the trickle of sweat that lodged between her breasts, until even the dog whines for home.

It ends like this: a downward curve of road past a crest of old cottages and a shabby field littered with the ruins of hen-runs where clipped strands of rusted wire fence the weeds in. To the left is the old estate where Joanie told me the woman locked her daughter up and, to the right, the half-flattened walls of mud and rock that once formed two-roomed labourers' cottages. Among the debris and glass a few scraps of wallpaper have survived a decade of exposure beside a tumbled down chimney breast smeared in graffiti.

Only one cottage stands intact on the right of that last slope into the river valley, the back gable unchanged for a century while at the side and front a room seems to have been added on or rebuilt with each passing decade. The building splays out like a drunken footstep, all styles of brickwork with twists and unrelated curves and crevices. No neighbours are left to complain of by-laws, no building inspectors tramping the yard with measuring tapes and notebooks.

The road falls steeply then to a lone set of traffic lights, to the left of which most of what Joanie claimed was an old famine burial mound has been bulldozed to make space for a cramped terrace of Noddyland town houses piggybacking each other back up the slope. To the right, the carriageway veers up towards the old village, railings sealing off the narrow gorge where a stream crosses the last remaining meadow perched incongruously among the factories and roads and houses. Across the road only the pillars remain of the gates of the big house where Joanie claimed her great grandmother lived. Beside them a meat refrigeration plant hums under floodlights, the air circulating like a chilled hand among the upturned carcasses. And finally to the left, past a pub and then a half mile of twisted cemetery railings, the road leans back upwards into the city.

I know that junction and those lights. On nights that summer when the last of the pub traffic accelerated up the carriageway I stood with Joanie arguing among the broken saplings ensnared by wire on the traffic island.

'I'm not going back, I'm not!' she'd argue. 'I hate that house. My granny like a crooked beetle stalking the gaff. I'll sleep on a park bench or where it's dry under the bridge, but I'm not going back in there.'

One night she had snatched up my tie when we were dressing and hidden it among her clothes. She produced it there, and wrapping it through the wire mesh protecting a slaughtered cherry blossom, bound her hands to it, her bobbing hair lit by the glare of a dozen headlights. She turned her back on me, pressed against the wire and bit into the cold steel with her teeth. Car horns were beeping on both sides of us, shouts from open windows, heads turning in the back seats. I thanked God that the lights were green, knowing at any moment they would force the cars to stop.

What the hell was I doing within sight of her own house with a nineteen-year-old girl who was acting deranged? I banged my fist against my forehead and looked around, thinking of escape.

'You're a crazy bitch,' I suddenly shouted. 'Sleep wherever you want. What the hell do I care?'

The lights turned red. A blonde in a low-cut dress was staring at us from a Volvo. I could read her lips as she spoke to the woman in the passenger seat.

'You fucked me, didn't you?' Joanie shouted over her shoulder.

'I wasn't the first.'

'Or the best.'

I stepped in front of the Volvo before the lights changed. I was half-way across when I glanced back. I could see Joanie's face peering through the long strands of brown hair, her eyes suddenly terrified at being abandoned. I couldn't move. I didn't want to go back but could not leave her. The lights turned green and the cars on the inner lane began to speed past. I shook my head and started to grin. She smiled back, exaggerating her bonded posture. The blonde beeped on her horn. I jumped out of her way as the car took off, both driver and passenger glaring back.

'No more blonde than my arse,' Joanie said. 'I bet you she had a black box bigger than an aeroplane.'

I could feel headlights sweeping over me as I laughed. It felt like those old films about escapees cornered between the barbed wire fences of a prison camp.

'You're going home, do you hear, and no more nonsense.'

She nodded her head.

'I can't untie myself.'

I loosened my tie and we kissed, a rare event in public. She fixed her black skirt and we walked up the far side of the hill together, gradually moving apart as we neared the windows of her granny's cottage. She crossed the road in front of me without glancing back. I walked on towards the crest of the hill and stopped in the shadow of an old wall. I lit a cigarette. Below me in the dip near the river I could see the ruins of other big houses, the roofs long stripped for lead, the walls tumbled in, trees growing in the windows, an old notice on a wall protesting at some local factory closure. I wondered how long it would be before they were cleared for yet another row of dinky town houses. It was hard to imagine anybody wanting to live at that halfway point between the city and nowhere. Security vans criss-crossed the industrial estate on the far hill. Six minutes passed before the door of the cottage opened and Joanie's little sister emerged, sleepy-eyed as if bribed to leave her bed. She glanced at the darkened window of her granny's bedroom, then ran down past the traffic lights and swung left towards the all-night garage opposite the cemetery. She was nine years of age. Her sneakers made no sound as I watched her fade into a blob under the ranks of amber lights. She was no concern of mine but I always waited till she came back, breathless, clutching crisps and chocolates for herself and, in their anonymous black cases, three horror videos for Joanie to sit up and watch.

★   ★   ★

I was born at the tail-end of a famine. Not the great one, just a minor, local affair where only scores died. Wasted bodies of children wrapped in sackcloth being carried by fathers past the cabin where my mother cried with the pain of birth. McAndrew, the landlord's agent, offered transportation to St John's in Newfoundland. My father brought us as far as the quayside in Sligo, queued with his neighbours in the sleet and looked at the ship.

'I'd sooner sink to hell than sail in that,' he told McAndrew.

'You're welcome to hell,' McAndrew spat back, 'and every last cottier with you.'

My father came closer to hell than his neighbours to Newfoundland. Cholera broke out when they had put to sea only eight days. Over half were dead, dumped at night overboard, before they sighted land again. Famished children with blue, wind-lashed faces staring back at the waves where their parents' corpses rode. Three times the ship tried to land, three times she was driven off. The captain died, two sailors who tried to swim for shore were shot by guards on the beach. They anchored on an island off the coast. A priest came out in a rowing boat and blessed them standing up while his oarsmen steadied the craft. The few remaining neighbours knelt, calmed by the sight of him like Jesus on the water. He gave a sign and the oarsmen began to pull, his hands still making the sign of the cross until their cries were no louder to him than the screeching of sea birds.

Hell, on the other hand, was dark as a rabbit burrow, twelve of us in an attic with a shattered skylight stuffed with papers to keep the rain out. Below in the streets ran creatures dressed in the scrapings of a dozen garments, battered top hats, skirts, anything that would shield them from the cold. Dublin was an alley-way with a million starving faces which I was led through clutching my sisters' skirts. An old woman with a bottom lip like a bloated crimson eel, a man missing his chin who swayed back and forth in a doorway. My mother pined for the sky above Sligo, my father for the plot he'd once rented, coming home late from other men's fields to tend his own few yards of rock and soil. My brothers pined for food, my sisters to grow upwards and out and become the wives of soldiers. I pined for a white space, somewhere clean, a corner without noise or clutter, where I might not be threatened or made to feel small.

Hegerty lived on the landing below us with a whole room to himself crammed with books and a black cloak he hung up carefully whenever he entered the house. He donned it again to tutor the offspring of shopkeepers, walking miles back from their houses to his own room, cursing any child who made a noise outside his door. Below us in a passageway he held a tiny school for scholars, a shed with half a door and barely light to make the print out. He hounded the street to seek pupils, to beat the outline of Latin and Greek into their heads. Those parents who could afford to paid, mostly he earned money by writing letters for strangers.

When I saw his door ajar I would creep in, in awe of

the space of it, the luxury of being able to stretch out your hands. Often Hegerty would look up and roar, sometimes he just nodded and I could linger.

Outside on the landing knots of older boys fell down the steps, screaming and wrestling like a tattered octopus. I could hear the shouts of my brothers, stronger than me, real men of twelve and thirteen bursting on to the street below. I was lost among such a crowd, a tongue-tied stutterer, a weak coward. I joined in only when they had taunted me to, as lost among that cluster of limbs as I was desperate to merge into them. That's how I remember myself, bare feet slipping on the cobbles as I tried to keep up with the crowd, a thin snail of snot eternally lingering on my lip as I shuffled along in the cold.

Only once did I prove my courage to them, on a December night when the light filtered in a dozen colours through the high stained windows of the Black Church.

'Three times around that and you'll meet the Devil,' an older boy cried. A carriage had stopped outside, a Protestant lady late for service. The boy ran with a scream once around it and then twice as we watched. He slowed, then ran on, weaker now, before gathering speed and suddenly turning to race away towards the canal leading into Broadstone station.

'He was that close,' an impressed youth whispered. 'What if he couldn't have stopped and Lucifer had sucked him in?'

Suddenly I surged forward and began to run. I could

hear the shouts of derision and then the warnings from my brothers. But I felt eerily calm as I ran. I was not strong or good at thieving, but I did not have to be. Because I now knew who I was going to be, the boy who had run to meet the Devil. Twice around I went and I could see their blurred faces, my brothers being held back, their mouths opening and closing. But I heard nothing except my blood pounding. I would never again need to hide in a corner, never fear a kick on the landing once I'd met the Devil. On the next corner I'll meet him, I told myself, on the next and the next. How often did I circle that church, the solemn organ playing, a huddle of terrified boys watching. 'Where are you?' I kept beseeching, as the world spun white and spacious and warm and remote.

When I came to they were crowded in a circle, bleached faces with awed expressions. 'What did he look like?' they asked. I should have felt pride, but I just knew disappointment and the same monotonous hunger. I said nothing on the way home as they jostled around me. Hegerty's door was open. He stood surprised at our silence.

'I saw the Devil,' I told him.

'What did he look like?'

'He was all white empty space,' I said. 'Empty space waiting to be filled.'

What was it about the mobile libraries that summer? The half-cracked spinster who had pottered around in charge for centuries was sick and a peaceful anarchy blossomed in her absence. The public service embargo had lasted so long we had all grown sick of one another's faces. Then suddenly in one month Joanie and three other school-leavers were thrust in among us. The yard thrived on their youth and life, drivers waylaying girls with buckets of water, impromptu singsongs on the vans we were meant to be cleaning. The trucks were battered blue antiques, throbbing out filthy diesel fumes, freezing cold in winter. The office was a lean-to built on to the front of an old warehouse that smelt of wax and dankness and had a cellar door leading down through a grim network of passageways to the city's sewers.

That summer every other girl there seemed to wear jeans, pastel shades so delicate one could trace the curve of panties as they climbed up into the vans. On the morning Joanie started work I had thrown the issue on board with the fine box we never used and the handful of reserved books, when Billy the driver came out with Joanie behind him dressed in a long loose black dress.

'Mind yourself,' Billy said as he stood back to let her climb in. She gathered the dress in her hand as she put her foot on the step, then swung her other leg forward up into the van. We both caught the brief flash of a white stocking top marking out a ridge of pale flesh bordered by a suspender. Billy whistled.

'Will I be safe with the pair of you?' she said, kneeling on the driver's seat to look down at us. Billy ruffled my hair as we climbed up to join her.

'You will with me, but this lad won't be if he starts wearing them yokes.'

She settled herself down on the long passenger seat, her shoes kicked off, legs already up on the dashboard touching the glass. Billy winked at me as I squeezed in beside her.

'I never wear jeans or tights,' she said, 'I hate them. They're not . . .' She paused for the right word. 'Victorian.'

There were four drivers in all but it was understood that Billy and I were a team together. He was bald and short and just the wrong side of fifty. A Scot who shared a spotless apartment with a lover, Graham, who sometimes came down to the yard. Watching them confer on something, I found it hard to imagine them making love. I just knew they would do it quietly and very slowly, with great tenderness and humour.

For a library assistant to be trapped inside the office on a summer's day was torture, to be out on a van paradise. That first morning Billy drove us to Portrane and Donabate. Victorian turned out to be Joanie's favourite word, used for everything she liked. The instant old wooden pubs we passed with the plastic signs and red leather seats still in a skip on the pavement outside, the Madonna-style outfits in the magazine in her hand.

We stopped at Corballis Cross, a lone golfer searching for his ball in a bush behind us, the sea broken by the old Martello tower. The battered kettle steamed on the rickety stove, Billy made tea in chipped mugs, then we settled down to playing cards, the deals broken by the occasional elderly borrower. Joanie had a way of laughing that involved her whole body, she would tell the bluest jokes for hours before her face suddenly succumbed into a scarlet blush. At one o'clock we scrambled over the rocks and walked along the beach together. Who began the play-acting I'm not sure, but suddenly the three of us were shaking sand from our hair. We ran between the tufts of grass on the dunes, ambushing each other on those concealed sandy hollows. I stumbled and she caught me by the neck, shovelling sand down my shirt before racing shrieking away. Billy had been left a little way behind us. I watched her scramble up the slope and stumble at the top just before I caught her. She twisted from me and we tumbled together, her legs cool against my arms, her face close with short excited breaths. I landed on top. Her dress had ridden up to reveal white suspenders and the palest of pink knickers flecked with fine grains of brown sand. We looked at each other without moving, her eyes serious and yet mocking, defying me to do something. I glanced up. Billy was watching us from the crest of the dune.

'Is it that time already?' he said softly and turned to walk back.

Even the trams have been extended this far. Two horses draw them to the bridge over the Tolka where a third is harnessed by the wall of the Botanic Gardens to pull the tramcar up the glistening slope of Washerwoman's Hill to its terminus. We are quite a growing township here. When I walk down to buy the *Dublin Evening Mail* Barre, the grocer, raves on about the extravagance of asphalting the paths and removing the mud heaps. 'Four shillings and sixpence per yard,' he shouts, thumping his fist on the counter. 'What sort of outlay is that for a poor township like ours?' The well-gravelled path did in his father's time.

I leave him there fingering his huge moustache, one eye peeled for carts turning out of Slut's Alley, and I think of my own father as I walk up the hill towards home. He too has come up in the world, his own stone cross, even if bought by me years later, with the inscription he could not have read in the great cemetery which shares this parish's name. Often in my head I try to tell him of my world, imagining his wonder at each invention, each new technical term. How far away famine seems from here, how distant three decades have become. We live in an age of science and change, of certainty and strength. I tell him this in my head as I walk, reassuring him that the hunger he dreaded for his family has long passed.

I own my own cottage between the barracks and the model school, within sight of the last street light beside the convent wall. Already I can see my daughter, white and blue in her Sunday dress, coming through fields of poppies to the banks of the Tolka. My profession is secure – the world will always need Latin and Greek. As long as I remain subservient and decorative the rich will find no reason to dispense with me. The future is bright as a shining new penny. So why do my talks with my dead father always become attempts to reassure myself?

Beyond the tram terminus the fields resume, the old coach road cutting through them down to the bridge. On the right a row of new labourers' cottages – Bridget's father's among them – stone walls and slate roofs looking down on the third-class cabins with mud walls nearer the river bank. Across from it the mound where the poor buried their famine victims, often still breathing, in open pits outside the railings of the new municipal city of the dead stretching down to the river. Next to it a tavern plies its trade, and across from that, by the walls of the asylum, the great wood begins. The small stream which gives that place its name can be glimpsed trickling down a gully through the trees by the roadside. Beyond the woods a second asylum appears, although the residents of our larger houses prefer to describe it as a rest home for patients of the upper and middle classes suffering from alcoholic excesses and other disorders. It boasts extensive pleasure grounds and views over the city. A fife and drum band march on Sundays to the indifferent stares of its inmates. But do not pass its gates. Turn left through the woods instead, cross the stream at Savages Lane to where the estate of Shallon House, the townland of the gallows, begins.

In my first days there I thought often of Hegerty and my father, their rows in that tenement over my weak frame. It began with the overwhelming whiteness of the first pages I glimpsed. The other boys left me alone after the Black

Church, ridiculing me but yet slightly afraid. I enjoyed my difference. I could turn Hegerty's leather covers in peace, run my palm over the smooth, unevenly cut pages. The print represented nothing except a strange reassuring order. It fitted each page, proportioned, complete. When I closed my eyes the black letters lingered, soothing me as if the noise of boys and the smells and shouts of the house were filtered out.

One day Hegerty's hand touched my shoulder. I looked up. He had risen from the table, was staring down at me.

'Can you read?'

'No.'

'Then what can you see?'

'It's perfect, Sir . . . like it contains everything.'

'What language is it?'

'The language of books, Sir. Different from what we speak.'

'What age are you, boy?'

'Almost eight and a half, Sir. Soon Dada says I'll be ready for work.'

'You know where my school is. Come to me there in the morning.'

'But my Dada says . . .'

'Be there or I'll split your blasted Dada's head open.'

I have never rid myself of the smell of that house. Sometimes when I bathe I still stop and sniff. Rain came in the smashed fanlight, ceilings that were once painted now flaked away into white chalky dust. Even as I ran upstairs my exhilaration vanished. Irish was a language spoken by my parents behind our backs. A backward trait which would drag us down if we caught a grasp of it. Only my mother relented, whispering half-daft stories we could barely follow on Sunday evenings. Books were objects which authority used to keep us in our place. My father's cramped room had space only for the functional English of the streets.

So I said nothing and retreated sullenly back into the tussle of limbs on the landing until the following evening when Hegerty's step silenced us. My brothers ran in to shelter, leering from behind my father's chair. They argued for half an hour while I listened out on the landing, the hordes of other children stomping up and down, the women slopping out their families or bent under buckets of water.

'The boy has to work like the rest of his kin. What future is there in this learning, what use is it for him at all?'

'The boy has words in his head, God blast you man. What class of labour will you find for him with thousands already out on the streets, old men before they are twelve?'

The door opened and Hegerty strode past me, down the stairs, not looking back. He slammed his own door and reluctantly I walked inside. My father sat at the chipped table, my brothers and sisters huddled now like a heap of rags on the bed. They looked at me already like I was a stranger. My mother fussed by the window, near tears and bewildered. The door behind me opened again. Hegerty stood glaring on the threshold. He flung the coins across the bare floor.

'There's as much as you'd earn from him labouring. He's hired out to me now. See you have him down early in the morning.'

The door shut and still nobody moved. The eyes and mouths of my brothers and sisters all formed three perfect Os. I knew my father wanted to smash the cracked plate before his hands. In Sligo he would not have been so easily conquered. McAndrew's cattle blinded with a knife the night after the agent drove two tenants off, a thirty-mile walk, when the famine was at its worst, for a day's relief work building a Government pier that crumbled back into the sea. Give him stones or bricks or human blood and he would deal with them. Here with Hegerty in the city he encountered words. He backed off, frightened of their closed secrets. He nodded at my mother who ran forward to gather up the money, thrusting a coin into my sister's hand, pushing her towards the door. The bundle of rags on the bed dispersed in an excited clamour like birds taking off. They pushed around me with shouts and laughter, giddy at the sudden prospect of food.

In the mornings Joanie would be the first to climb on to a van before the cleaners were off and, hogging the seat at the end, would take down a book on anything Victorian. Period romances, biographies of Prince Albert, books of old photographs gathering dust on the oversized shelves.

The girls restocked around her. If one dumped a pile of books beside Joanie she'd smile vaguely and look back at the sepia albums. Back in the office while the others pretended to look busy she'd vanish into the storeroom and rip the plastic covers off a few hardbacks. She'd smoke cigarettes taken with great display from a battered cigarette case, with the damaged books piled in front of her, only bothering to pick up the scissors or Sellotape when someone important entered.

'The girl has this job sussed already,' Billy claimed after a week. 'There are girls here ten years who are only trotting behind her.'

And he was right. She seemed without nerves or fear of anybody. Her mind was a polished stone focused just on what concerned her. Although I was only a decade older, in that office we seemed from distant generations. Put on or not, she had an air of having already seen more of life than the rest of us. And yet parts of her were childish, a constant boasting about her family's success, a way of walking as though the eyes of every man in the room couldn't leave her.

Only out on the vans did she open up, joke as we climbed into the cabin, throw her hair back and tease Billy as he drove. The rosters should have meant we were out together only occasionally, but after six years I knew how to twist them, and without any conscious plans I began to pair Joanie and myself together.

That first month we covered the whole of North Dublin;

every tiny seaport and rural village, secluded housing estates dropped as if by chance among fields of corn, children zigzagging across hillocks of muck like soldiers in the Great War to queue with books on the half-finished fringes of the city.

'You look jaded,' Billy shouted to her one morning as I leaned against the counter flap to hold on to a boiling kettle in the traffic.

'It's my sister,' Joanie said. 'She's only eighteen months. Drives me crazy at night with her crying. She's in with my parents but they sleep like logs.'

That lunch-time near Ballyboughal she told us about her home; the granny in the private geriatric hospital whom they visited on Sundays when her father, a sales manager based in London, was home. Her brother who had finished two years in London University, her elder sister who was training as a British Airways hostess. Billy rolled his eyes, impressed.

'How many younger than you?' he asked.

'Just the one. My little sister.'

'That's quite a gap.'

'So what if it is?' Joanie said and stared moodily out at the trees on the crossroads where we had hidden the van.

That night Billy offered to drop her at her door. We halted at the traffic lights at the end of the carriageway. Joanie pointed at the new town houses half-way up the hill.

'Daddy's car's there,' she said. 'He must be home.'

'They're new houses,' Billy said, 'I thought you had always lived here?'

'No, somewhere else,' Joanie replied, 'somewhere different.'

In the rear-view mirror I watched her shrink into a motionless black speck refusing to budge until we were gone.

We worked from dawn until the last light could be wrestled from the sky, then huddled over candles till my eyes ached as if needles were pushed through the pupils. Hegerty brought me through every volume on his floor, dismissive of English but accepting its purpose, lingering like an old miser with a naked girl over every closely printed phrase of Latin. He closed his school in the lane, made me wait in the rain outside the houses he tutored in, gibbering to me in Latin as we pushed our way home through the packed streets. I learnt fast and if I dozed a fist against the side of my skull reminded me of lessons undone. He wanted my attention for every word, thrilling in my grasp of pronunciation, reliving each fresh revelation of language through me again.

Late at night I would climb upstairs, fight for a space in the mass of bodies on the straw mattress in the corner. My brothers and sisters shifted grudgingly, greedy for space and warmth. I no longer belonged to them, felt their resentment even as they ate whatever scraps of food Hegerty's few coins brought in. They gave to each other while Hegerty taught me to withhold, to gather the strength to master the books and not fall asleep, risking a blow to my neck. He taught me Greek and Latin and how to be apart until even their derision did not register. I lived in a world without rich or poor, a sphere of cold and rigid letters.

When deep hunger visited the city Hegerty fed me scrapings without them knowing, when scarlet fever broke out he refused to allow me to return home. I shared his rough bed, felt the hard ridges of his bones dig into me as he slept, watched with him as three of my brothers were carried off in coffins tacked together from packing cases. For a fortnight we both starved on soup that was little more than water with pepper so he could buy me an old suit off the cobbles in the market. Now I followed him into homes in Phibsborough and Drumcondra, papists trying to cast off the accents of the poor, watched their dumb children stutter over my immaculate words. And always he spoke of me as his protégé, whispering urgently to bored parents on the doorsteps, searching for the scholarship that would make me secure.

From before dawn on Sundays till the last priest was unrobed he bundled me from front pew to front pew, dressed in my worst rags, a Latin missal held up in my hands.

'These bastards in the skirts have the power now,' he'd mutter, smiling meekly when one of them glanced down at us from the altar. The reputation he spread grew. I acquired rumours of a vocation before the first stirrings of hair on my body. The priests took me in tow, paid for schooling, university at sixteen, a plot for my father when he died, a dinner in my honour when I graduated with distinction. From a devout bundle of rags in a pew to a priest robed in his finery. What an example to the poor, what an exhibit to be displayed before visiting prelates. They raised their glasses and smiled, beckoning gently towards the seminary.

I went to Hegerty for advice, careful on the stairs lest I meet my mother or her two daughters who were still unmarried. His skin was jaundiced and stretched on his jaws. He spat out yellow spittle mixed with the hint of blood.

'Run like the clappers of hell from the bastards,' he said and coughed half his insides up.

'How can I thank you?'

'I've a plot long bought in Glasnevin. You buy me a tombstone, boy, and make sure you inscribe it in perfect Latin.'

The clergy do not like to be cheated. No school would open its doors to me, no Catholic home risk the possibility of their disapproval. And that is how I came to Shallon House, a rarity, a dancing bear, a token poor papist with knowledge. My employers liked me to appear at their parties so guests could marvel at their benevolence. My smile was pitched just above that of a servant's. I quoted a few phrases and disappeared like a dog that has been patted. Often outside on the lawn leading down to the gate-lodge and woods I would smash my fist in my palm and curse them in every useless language as the waltzes began, the swirl of white skirts at windows. My cell-like room above the servant quarters beckoned. I belonged to no one, stripped of the hungers of my class and given ones no feast could satisfy. If language could smash walls I would have razed that house. Instead I looked around for something to subvert them, to be master of. It was then, one morning, that I saw Bridget.

Most afternoons in the office I went for a sleep upstairs in the storeroom, stretched out on the dusty bench beside the old encyclopaedias and the rare Y stock. One Wednesday I heard footsteps on the wooden stairs and leaned forward, waiting to spring to work when they reached my bay. They turned down the next bay and stopped. Joanie's eyes leaned down to stare across the open-backed shelves.

'Is this Aladdin's cave?' she asked. 'I want a guided tour.'

I beckoned and began to show her my favourite old books: *Forbidden and Suspect Societies* from the Catholic Truth Society on the dangers of the Young Men's Christian Association and Rotary Clubs; hotel brochures promising flushing water closets and running water; the Revd Caswell's *Guide for Young Females of the Middle Classes to be a Model Victorian Wife*.

'There should be one somewhere here,' I said, 'written by an ancestor of mine. My great grandfather, some class of a Latin scholar but I'm not sure of his surname. *Tales of the West of Ireland* or some such lark. My grandmother had a copy but they threw it out when she died.'

Joanie wasn't listening. Her face lit up as she pored over the ragged cut pages of Caswell's *Guide*, pausing at the drawings of clothes and household plans and the photos of carriages.

'I was born too late for all that,' she said sadly.

I climbed up and pulled down more dust-covered books, infant mortality statistics and comparisons of Dublin and Calcutta by foreign travellers.

'It wasn't all coaches and pretty maids and glamour,' I said. 'It was pretty poxy for most of our ancestors.'

'Not for me it wouldn't have been.' Joanie was suddenly vehement. 'I'd have had my own set of rooms and a maid to do my bidding, a carriage with two black horses waiting and a gentleman to offer me cigarettes from a gold case.'

'What if you were born poor?'

'I was born poor in this life, but I wouldn't stay poor back then. I'd have all the things I'd want and if he couldn't give me them I'd leave him for another who could.'

'Who?'

She snapped the book shut as I suddenly thought of her father's town house and company car.

'I'd find the richest man in this filthy city and I would make sure I became his best mistress.'

Two years had passed in Shallon House before that morning. For days afterwards I watched her, lifting the trays in the morning-room, walking through the walled kitchen garden towards the servants' door, running, and then when she realized she was being observed, walking to answer the cook's shouts from downstairs.

There was nothing special to mark Bridget out for me and yet I developed a quiet, almost morbid, fascination with her that I found hard to shake off. I had little to interest a woman, a tutor from my background is between classes. To those who can match my education I may perhaps be an amusing companion but can never hope to be more. To those hardened girls of the lower orders, who smell of the cramped tenements that cling like an invisible stain to me, I have the manners of a gentleman with none of the money and position which go with them. Although here 'the manners of a gentleman' is a meaningless phrase. The rich stave off boredom inside their houses circled by trees like a peasant fights hunger. Outside their drawing-rooms they have no more manners than any of their tenants' pigs. I have seen one of them out hunting use his whip on the boy Turlough who had fallen in his bare feet down Watery Lane almost in front of their horses' hooves. I say nothing, my job is to teach their offspring, be the occasional object of philanthropic voyeurism from their guests and otherwise keep my mouth shut.

The question still haunts me. Why, from the morning when I had leaned from my window to see Bridget vainly knocking on the front door, growing more desperate as the moments passed and nobody answered, had I known that she would be the first woman whose limbs would open beneath my own?

It was her prolonged knocking that morning which had woken me. I lay perplexed for a moment. In my time there I had never known anybody knock more than once on the front door. Often if I descended the stairs quietly I'd catch O'Rourke, the butler, in the alcove beneath the staircase with all his other work finished and his eyes trained on the bulk of the oak door, his bent frame poised like a race horse's awaiting the starter's flag. For all I know he may have slept that way, certainly I believe he spent hours in that posture, shuffling away only if somebody spied him. When the door was eventually pounded upon he never moved at once, he waited, visibly restraining himself for the length of time it would have taken him to walk from his small office beside the kitchens, and then set forth at an almost boyish trot down the waxed hallway. Watching from the stairs, one could gauge the caller's stature by the angle to which O'Rourke's whole trunk descended. But after long observation I realized that his head always began its descent before the door was fully opened and he could possibly have glimpsed the caller. I decided that years of hovering in the musty alcove had awakened a sixth sense within him, that he could not only distinguish between knocks, but knew, before a carriage had stopped or boots mounted those twelve steps, who each caller was and, for all I know, the exact nature of their business.

I lay that morning between the sheets, watching thin slats of light intensify as they squeezed through the gaps in the shutters. My first thought was that O'Rourke had died –

mere illness would never have been sufficient to cure his obsession for servitude. But surely that in itself would not necessitate the superbly orchestrated machine of the house capitulating into chaos. His remains would pass out the back door with no more fuss than those of a finished meal and someone else who took size nine shoes would be appointed to open the door and break in his master's footwear.

I crossed the room to pull open the wooden shutters and lean out. A maze of curled hair confronted me and then an upturned face with frightened eyes as Bridget looked up, distracted by the noise of my window. She looked nineteen, if that, obviously a girl from the village or the new labourers' cottages built near the bridge below the wood. She was close to tears, like a child struggling with a foreign language or a savage baffled by the most rudimentary mechanism. With another I would have been tempted to laugh at her ignorance, yet with her something fascinated me from the first glance. Partly it was the fear in her eyes that was caused not just by the predicament she found herself in, though that was the reason for her present terror. But it was as if that terror was a manifestation of a deeper, ingrown horror which remained constantly just below the surface. That I realized later, but at the moment when I leaned down to observe the look of helplessness and the search for reassurance in her face what I felt most was a strange sense of absolute power as though I could mould this frightened figure into anything that I wished.

You should not imagine that as a tutor I am a man well

versed in power. My charges were then aged thirteen and eleven respectively, their characters already formed as surely as if lava had slid across the nursery while they slept and hardened into rock around their white skin. For all my temporary power, my lists of Latin verbs and algebraic equations, they knew that this learning was really a game, an exercise to lend a veneer of sophistication to the stark, pure power of their money, just as they knew that the right word to their father would cast me out from the sanctuary of that single room I was then allowed to call home.

'What are you doing, girl?' I called down.

'It's the door, Sir, nobody will answer it to me. Surely there are people inside?'

I could imagine the deserted alcove where O'Rourke normally stood. The knock would have startled him like an apparition from the underworld, no creak of a carriage wheel, no thud of a well-heeled boot on the gravel. It would take him a moment to realize that the unmentionable had happened and then he would be gone, slipping down the dark passageway to his office, knowing nobody would have the audacity to approach the door in his absence, deeming it below himself to even reprimand the offender.

'What's the nature of your business, child?'

'Work, Sir. My father arranged it.'

'You're at the wrong door, child. Nobody will answer a servant there.'

It was so quick that I could not be sure I saw it, but an amused knowing smile seemed to cross her face as she glanced at the carved iron knocker, but when she looked back up at me her eyes were filled with the same confusion.

'Follow that gravel path around the side of the house till you reach a small door. That's where you must go.'

She turned and began to run across the wet grass to the path, turning back flustered to thank me again and almost falling as she did so. I watched her run in short, frantic strides and found myself piecing together her body beneath the heavy layers of clothes. As I withdrew my head I realized that my penis had stiffened slightly beneath my nightshirt. I lay back on the bed, watching the light play with the tall jug of water beside my shaving bowl, and longed for a cigarette to hold between my fingers.

I was edgy all that day, filled with a restless pent-up sense of expectation. Even my charges felt it. I was tolerated in that house because of a fashion, everybody had a tutor like a grandfather clock or the latest scarf from London. It had become a matter of spite for me to fill their heads with questions in the hope that some half-sown seed would somehow disrupt the impervious grind of the house in years to come. It is important for social stability for the landlords to remain as dumb as the tenants beneath them. But that morning they could have remained as ignorant as the savages in the Colonies for all I cared. I set them a stiff passage of Caesar to translate and left them to frown and make faces at each other across the polished wood. The window looked out on to the kitchen garden and part of the stone–flagged yard where the girls were hanging great white sheets out to dry. I wanted one glimpse to reassure myself that the girl had not been dismissed on the spot upon reaching the kitchen and then I swore to return my mind to the monotonous duties of the schoolroom. Each girl came forth in her uniform, sleeves rolled back as she carried the heavy basket and vanished back again behind the ivy-cluttered wall, leaving the sheets rippling like flags with water dripping down on to the stones. Behind me there was silence in the room as the children ceased to fidget and bicker and became genuinely alarmed at my indifference. All my moods they had grown used to, from forced humour to anger; the one thing their life had never prepared them for was to be ignored. Finally I felt my shirt being tugged, and I looked down into the worried eyes of the youngest who held her exercise book aloft to be examined. I smiled and for the first time ever received an honest smile of affection in return. As I turned from the window back to my duties a figure emerged briefly in the courtyard below, and though there was nothing in the uniform to distinguish her from the others, I knew instinctively it was Bridget and it stirred something in me that she had not been dismissed, as if a small spark of rebellion had been lit, even by accident, and had survived in the ordered conformity of that house.

The next night was pay-night, another tacky Thursday in the basement of a pub, two dozen library assistants intent on blowing a fortnight's wages. The dance floor was the width of a phone box, the bar a hatch poked out in the wall. The whole joint had a seedy magic, the toilets a descent to a dungeon of cracked enamel and small round cakes of detergent that smelt of piss, where footsteps clattered on the jigsaw of hammered glass that served as a skylight in the ceiling.

I was smoking small, tipped cigars, drinking pints, trying to convince a new girl that Billy was the City and County Librarian.

'The City and County Librarian's a woman,' she kept protesting and Billy would strut his chest out and wink.

'She's fierce butch all the same,' I'd say to the girl who looked increasingly worried.

It was near closing time when I met Joanie at the bar.

'Where's the most beautiful girl in the libraries been keeping herself?' I was joking but I could see her sudden pleasure. She was buying cigarettes and emptying them into the gold case she always carried around. I accepted one and fingered the battered case.

'Very sophisticated,' I said, 'Victorian. It suits you down to the ground.'

She smiled like a little girl dressed up in her mother's shoes. That's how I thought of her at that moment, playing at being an adult. The barmen were still serving drink even as they called out time. We began to dance in the ruck of bodies under the single spotlight, Billy watching, amused as he guarded our drinks at the table, girls around him arguing about whose flat they would invade to party in.

Without warning, Joanie began to give me a seemingly endless French kiss. Whenever my eyes wandered around the floor she would sense it and, easing her tongue back a fraction, whisper for me to concentrate. I felt pleasurably helpless, knowing that she was publicly claiming me, that she knew how the eyes of every library assistant were now focused on the arch of her neck bent back beneath my lips. Even when the music stopped and the other dancers cleared away she held her posture, playing for time perhaps or just waiting till she was ready.

Finally she withdrew her lips.

'Have you a place to stay?'

'There'll probably be a party,' I said.

'Have you a place?'

I nodded.

'Fuck their party so.'

She paused only twice. Once to get our coats and glasses while I bargained for a bottle of vodka at the bar, and again, for a second at the door with the glasses hidden by her bag, half glancing back as if listening to silent applause. Outside I tried to take her hand.

'I never hold hands,' she said. 'It feels like someone owning me.'

We walked up along the quays towards my flat, finishing off our drinks. I still could not quite believe what had happened, kept waiting for her to make some excuse and leave. I was excited at the prospect of sex and yet, in those tumbledown alley-ways still glistening after a fall of rain, I felt an abundant tenderness towards her curious innocence. I would have been happy to have just sat on the edge of those damp cobbles with my arm around her. If Joanie felt that serenity she seemed threatened by it. She needed to talk incessantly, stories I could hardly believe about the men she had known, prison officers and soldiers, two-timing, three-timing them, being sneaked in the windows of Cathal Brough barracks, getting back over walls before dawn.

'If I were a man,' she said, 'you'd admire me for it. You'd think I was a bit of a lad, so tell me why shouldn't a girl have fun as well?'

We were passing the lane where the mobile vans were parked. An old woman in a crooked hat was feeding the wild cats who lived among the rotten beams of abandoned buildings on the quay.

'What about your parents?' I asked. 'Do you not have to be in?'

'They don't care what I do. They let me live my own life. Really, I can do anything I want.'

Was she frightened of affection or did she just want a one-night stand? I thought of my flat, wished I had made the bed before I went out.

'Even cook breakfast?'

'Are you looking for a mistress,' she said, 'or a maid?'

The old woman had moved back into the shadows. I placed Joanie's empty glass in mine and flung them high over the gates of the yard. They shattered near the steps of the office startling the cats who scattered underneath the vans. She had set the agenda.

'Race you home,' I said and began to run.

There were items of her clothing she wanted me to remove and others she refused to allow me to touch. She was slightly dumpy when she was naked, her words spoken with quiet dramatic pausing.

'I tell every man I sleep with the same. You can do anything you want. I mean it. Anything.'

'Do you want me to wear something, a condom?'

'What kind of girl would ask a man to do that?' she replied, genuinely shocked.

To reach my flat we had had to climb over stacks of the cheap furniture which the landlord, who owned the bargain shop underneath with the permanent *Closing Down Sale* sign, stored in the hallway. The late-night disco in the hotel next door thumped away like a distant rhythmic poltergeist. She was not the prettiest of the few girls I had known, and for all her talk seemed to have little idea of what to do with her body, yet I have never remained as hard for so long with any other woman. She came quickly with a short intake of breath, then focused her attention on me.

'I never come more than once before my man,' she said. 'Now relax, I'll help you, relax.'

And yet I couldn't come. I could hear couples emerging from the nightclub and hailing taxis on the quay. A fight started between the bouncers and a Chinese youth. Cars slowed down or moved off shifting panes of light across the ceiling.

'It's not fair, for me to give everything I have and you to hold back.' Joanie sounded genuinely upset. 'I want to share with you, give you back pleasure in return.'

But still I tensed up inside as Joanie broke her rule about coming again and again. I had never known a woman like that before, never felt the strange sense of power she seemed to want to make me feel I had. When I finally came it was with a quiet ache of relief, the pleasure of it muted by what had already passed. Joanie lay under me as if shot, her hair drenched on the pillow, and whispered that no man had ever done that to her before.

It is curious how when you close your eyes during the final moments of sex you often visualize other things, a train careering down a tunnel, familiar faces flashing past into the dark. Like the final moments of your life perhaps. I lay beside her, not remembering people but the distance between them.

I have never felt myself better than those I grew up among, just different. Perhaps it was being the youngest of a family with a ten-year gap. The working class who made good in the early seventies, who left the tech at sixteen and wound up senior civil servants and marketing directors. How many Saturday evening parties in their houses, older people, older music, myself at twelve or thirteen awkward in a corner, my parents at sixty, proud but bewildered in another? Somehow I had never connected, with them or much else that came later.

I had lived with my parents in the Ballymun flats then. At six each morning I would run out through the country lanes to St Margaret's. If I was lonely I fought it by imagining myself somehow marked out, that among those fields where white mist hung a revelation waited. I ran hard towards it, pure in my strength and youth. And somehow I have always remained that boy, still chasing purity, still on the threshold of some great event. I was spoiled at that early age; every morning I rendezvoused with my own god on those damp roads, his feet beat with my footsteps on the hard tarmacadam, his breath panted with mine in the half-light. Maybe that's why nothing ever seemed important afterwards, work, money, women. All were traps to be avoided. I needed to be free to keep my destiny. I grew older but never changed. I was careful, avoided interviews for promotion, group savings schemes, the eyes of girls in work with suburban minds primed to pay off a mortgage for half their lifetime.

The only thing I had not bargained for was ageing. Part of me hates to admit that I can be lonely. But at that moment with Joanie I realized how stale my life had become. It felt so good to be close to her, so drained and so secure. The tenderness I had known in the laneway came back and this time Joanie seemed to share it. I knew I would never hold out so long again, knew that I had surrendered my trust to her.

We slept and woke with the city snarling below us, traffic inching like an angry glacier along the quay. We breakfasted quietly in a small Italian coffee shop near Christchurch and separated at the entrance to the lane leading up to the yard.

Joanie went ahead and I followed a few seconds behind. As I turned in the gate I saw the squad car parked outside the office window. I felt a flush of guilt, glancing at the smashed glasses on the ground. A Garda was talking to Joanie. Billy grinned from the door of his cab.

'You're lucky the US marines didn't come crashing in the window of your flat.'

I looked at him and he pointed at the Gardai climbing back into their squad car.

'Our lady friend has a granny who doubles as an all-in wrestler. Half past two last night she was on the phone to every librarian in the city threatening hellfire if her granddaughter wasn't immediately delivered home.'

'Joanie's granny is in an old folks' home. She lives with her parents.'

'Her parents are stiffs up in Glasnevin cemetery. The girl lives with her granny and not in those town houses, according to the police, but that old cottage across from them.'

Joanie had vanished inside. The girls climbing up to tidy Billy's van grinned as they passed us.

'Does everybody know where she was?'

'Come on kid, yourself and Queen Victoria were hardly discreet.'

★　　★　　★

A big house is like a clerk's office in a novel by Dickens – to an outsider, high windows and silence broken only by the busy hum of work, but for those within the very walls seem alive with whispered secrets. Bridget's mother had died in a fire when she was a child, this much I gleaned merely by passing doorways where undermaids stooped at their work. She lived alone with her father in the new cottages near the bridge. He worked nights in season in the new mill at Cross Guns and sometimes took work at Shallon when the milling was slack.

Lingering in a corridor I heard the cook discuss the death of her mother. 'Only four or five she was, alone with the charred corpse all night. Do you think she was crying when her father found her in the morning? She was just staring about the room, didn't even speak to anyone for days afterwards.'

Why had her mother taken her out of the bed that night? Was she lonely perhaps, a bride left alone thinking of her husband, his face white as a death mask, hauling sacks of flour to the hoist? Nobody ever knew what had happened, they say her mother must have stumbled at the hearth, perhaps building the fire up with turf. There was a wound where her forehead struck the stone. They could still discern the outline of it though most of her skin was burnt. The hair must have caught hold first, a crackling, licking noise, a sickening smoulder giving way to the first yellow spurt of flame. For some reason her clothes had not taken aflame. Her nightdress was white, untouched, modestly shielding her legs when they found her, her belly betraying the fact that she was six months pregnant. The floor was stone. The fire had flickered its own way out. Bridget could walk but they felt that she had never moved all night, her legs splayed in front of her, her body upright, her eyes never ceasing their orbit of the room. There seemed nothing the cook did not know about that night; Bridget's father arriving home, the smell in his nostrils, neighbours crowding in the door behind him. O'Rourke was almost upon me before I heard his footsteps. He passed on to the kitchen with the curtest of nods and the cook stopped talking.

Was it coincidence that I seemed to glimpse Bridget every time I passed through the house? Kneeling on the stairs to scrub each step, scurrying down passageways as if frightened of the very furniture, peering out through a window at her mistress preening on the lawn like an elaborate parasolled scarecrow. Always I felt I had just missed a slight raising of her eyes before she slipped away. My mind began to play tricks. I felt that if I did not pass her on each journey some misfortune would befall, began to wonder *was she too looking out for me?* I could not describe the fevered things I dreamt of at night: her body whiter than white against the grained wood of the master's study and every thrust of our limbs a desecration of the crystal glass and marble floors built on thousands of deaths. It was like a virus let loose inside me, without reason to it as it took over my life.

Each day I heard some new whisper from the parlour-maids about her, that she was odd, half demented, always whispering to herself. Her eyes looked jaded as though she never slept and that same troubled look never left her like a vague foreboding that could not be shaken off.

My lessons finished early. From four o'clock I was my own master, expected only to keep out of people's way. Often I would explore the attics; trunks of abandoned clothes and lives, a scamper of rats, the same curious rich melancholy as in a graveyard at evening. I am not sure who was the most startled when I came across her there, and who was the least surprised. She had a trunk open, was kneeling with both arms sifting through the musty garments. She looked back over her shoulder at the noise of my footfall, a slight smile on her face, her eyes staring past me for a moment. Then she coloured as if naked and rose, dusting her uniform as she pushed past. She pushed the door open and ran, the hinges swinging back and forth after her.

That night I dreamt that I woke, knowing she was there kneeling before the trunk. I walked from my room down the unlit corridors. I opened the attic door without speaking. I told myself it was a dream, tried to wake myself up but I could not. The grey moonlight slanted through the narrow skylights. The only noise was that of bats whirling between the rafters above us. I bolted the door behind me. She lay across the trunk, her knees on the bare boards, the white promise of calf exposed. Her face was serious but yet again I felt I had just missed a smile, that if I turned my eyes away her gaze would mock me. She never raised her head as she followed my instructions mutely, the garments slowly taken from her shoulders, the dress and then petticoats lowered and stepped from, the stays loosened, the skin revealed. When she was naked we stood facing each other. Her long hair obscured her face as she knelt before me, drawing me out briefly into the moonlight and down the shafting tunnel of her throat. Her teeth were sharp when she touched against it, her tongue seeming to buckle against the head, driving back the foreskin to cling against the knob, exposing the curved glans to her hot saliva. Often the shaft was buried in her throat, my hands in her hair as she almost choked on its length, then only the tip of her tongue would run lightly over the head. My legs began to go from me as I felt the spasm begin and suddenly it had become her turn to play master. She pinched the base of my penis sharply and held it between her finger and thumb on the throbbing vein as I tried to dislodge her. I put my hand down to block hers and she squeezed my balls tightly, forcing me to cry out. I sank to my knees till we were even, face to face. Downstairs it was suddenly daylight. I could hear the household moving about their duties. She was not smiling. Her mouth opened under mine and she bit my tongue when it slid in.

'Fuck me,' she said, 'but fuck me when I tell you. Fucking Johnny tutor. Fucking Sligo dirt. You get me pregnant, Johnny tutor, I'll come after you with a knife, I'll cut your balls out. Remember that, tutor.'

She reached out and with her nails suddenly ripped the skin below my left eye. I could feel a tearing pain and hear her laugh at the blood on her fingers. The slap sent her reeling back on to the floor. She lay with her back turned, both hands held up to her face. I could not tell if I heard sobbing or laughter. She half rose on her haunches as if to crawl away but when I touched her hips with my arms she knelt as if frozen, her forehead pressed against the floorboards, her knees a bare foot apart. As I began to enter her she turned her head, sinking her teeth into the flesh just below my thumb to stop from crying out. We were sharing that pain now, the more I pushed into her the sharper her teeth clung to my flesh. There was blood on my hand, blood on my prick. It was like pushing my way into an impassable future, like piercing the weight of nothingness. My penis felt that it would snap. She lifted her head from my bleeding hand to shriek once – I did not know from pleasure or pain – a long drawn out howl like a dying animal. It seemed loud enough to fill the house and yet in the silence that followed with only the sounds of our breath and hearts, we could hear from below the same unconcerned noises of the house, a maid climbing the stairs in short obedient steps, men unloading wood in the courtyard below. The attic was cut off from its time and its world now, nothing we did or said in it could ever penetrate into the ordered twilight of those landings and stairs. When it was over I lay across her body and neither of us spoke. The bats blundered against the window. The light came and went as if days were flickering past like trees from a carriage window. There was the aftertaste of both pleasure and pain and yet I felt strangely numb. It was as if neither of us were the people we actually were, as if we were puppets forced to act in some child's game. The figure who lay beneath me, who had howled like some primeval animal, was this the girl whose vulnerability had attracted me just mornings before? And was I myself that timid tutor who had passed his days like a half-ghost half-monk wandering through those rooms below? I gazed down at our bodies and felt an overwhelming sorrow for us both. She stirred below me, dislodging my shrivelled penis, turned her face towards mine and whispered in that normal frightened voice of hers.

'It's still there, haunting me, it's not gone. God help me, oh, God help me, Sir.'

I woke drained and felt the dampness of my legs. I was filled with a terror I could not explain and yet filled with an excitement that was even more terrifying. If I believed in ghosts I would have sworn something evil was in the air. I pushed the window open. The air was cool, reassuring. Through the trees I could see the figure of Matthew, an old man who often slept out in the woods, staring towards me.

I wanted to avoid Bridget next day as if afraid to face her and yet I knew I would keep pacing the corridors, back-tracking, trying to fool myself that I needed things in rooms until I finally caught a glimpse of her. I was at a bend in the stairs when we passed. She blushed, lowered her eyes, hurried on. It was the trunk, I told myself, being caught going through it in the attic. She was ashamed, frightened I'd inform on her. Yet I couldn't shake the thought of what if her haste was more than that, if she knew of my dream, the thoughts in my head.

I couldn't sleep that night; lighting the candle, blowing it back out, listening for noises as though the room was unknown to me. I knew what I would have to do but kept trying to pretend that sleep would come instead. Eventually I rose and dressed, moved stealthily up the stairs to the attics, paused at the door as if uncertain whether to knock. What did I expect inside: answers, an end to this fever, a frightened girl waiting for me with her hair let down, a creature of breasts and claws luring me towards some unknown terror? I was no longer thinking straight. I pushed the door open. Dust, a filter of grey through the skylight, the solemn bulk of heavy trunks. I waited for hours there. I was no longer who I was, all the learning had slipped from me. Hegerty's language, the ice palace he had taught me to live within, the words priests had whispered in my ears, all of it had evaporated and what was left was that starving boy, bewildered in a street of screaming faces, knowing only an overwhelming hunger.

My work began to suffer. I knew it would not be long before it was noticed. But I drifted each evening from the house to the village. Being the occasion of excessive fighting and drinking the Humours of that village have long been banned. In May of each year a shaved and soaped pig had been let loose for men to try to catch, bell-ringers were caught by blindfolded men, yokels held grinning contests through horse collars, and smock races for serving girls were run. Only the May Pole remained now, a battered strip of wood with flaking blue and red stripes of paint. Outside the tavern where I drank the local youths threw pebbles at it as they crowded around the horse trough to leer at the serving girls coming in from the farms.

In the unlit smoky room inside the older men grunted their respect as I passed but they knew I was not gentry. Language was all that kept me above them, pull that magic rug of words and I would land beneath them, a cottier's son back in my proper station. The local ale was filthy, the local speech, at times to an educated ear almost a broken English, pronounced in a short and guttural manner. I'd wipe my lips and move out through the doorway, pausing at the bridge on Church Street to gaze down the valley past the woods to the city. There is good hunting there for rabbits and birds, often the trees were thick with shouts below Savages Lane. The young boy Turlough, who sometimes helped at Shallon, was often to be glimpsed, earning a farthing for carrying this or running with that. Old Matthew squatted among the trees in the dusk watching the young men at their sport. Some years back he was said to have brought the new rector to the very spot in the old graveyard where a local cross had been buried. I had tried to talk to him once but he just stared at me hunched down among the branches like an animal. Sometimes children stone him or a farmer stuck for labour has him stooped in a field. Mostly the villagers pay him no more heed than if he were some ancient plant rooted there in the ground.

I was biding my time, like a lover pacing the floor before a rendezvous. I'd check my timepiece, watch for the road to clear, try to saunter casually down through the summer dust of the road through the woods to the city, quickening my step when I was beyond the village, terrified she might leave early, then slow again, equally nervous at being seen waiting at the gap between the whitethorn hedges that bordered the gully down to the stream. I would stand back among the bushes and wait for her step, then dart forward and be climbing back up the road when she rounded the bend. I lived for that brief moment, knowing both ignominy and elation, catching my breath as her hair came into view. I never spoke, hurrying on as if going somewhere in haste. She would pass with a blush, lowering her head, her feet hastening beneath her petticoats till she was safely away.

One evening she must have taken a short cut through the woods. When I reached my spot she was there at the gap before me, staring at the cattle standing in the water below, their tails chasing the flies that bothered them. For all my obsession with her I never gave much thought to how she viewed me. I had felt myself somehow invisible to her, now I was shocked to see her there. I was almost past before her gaze stopped me. I was a tutor and she a serving girl, I told myself. I tried to hide my anxiety in a mannered voice.

'Who are you waiting for, child?'

'A gentleman with a gold case to offer me a cigarette.'

I laughed, waiting for her to smile, but her face was serious.

'And who would he be?'

'I do not know, but that is what I have always dreamt of.'

An old woman appeared from the cottage beside the stream and, with a glance up, scattered feed to the hens in her yard. Bridget's eyes followed her.

'What else do you dream of?'

'Things. I don't always understand them. Is your name Johnny?'

I laughed.

'Sean I was christened, but Johnny was what my father always called me. How did you know that?'

'I didn't but it suits you. *Johnny I hardly knew you.*'

She sang the line of the song with a curious childish lilt. I have always been used to guile in a young girl's voice. Bridget's openness frightened me somehow. A hay cart was coming up from the bridge, its driver unknown to me. She turned her head and stared at me.

'Why do you always wait here until I pass, Sir?'

I felt exposed suddenly, wanted to deny it. The cart creaked past us, the driver giving the horse the slightest flick of his whip. I could hear the sound of male voices shouting in the woods and a girl's laugh.

'Why don't you answer? I answered your questions. Have you read all the books up in the master's library?'

'All of them, no.' I laughed. 'Many are just minutes of civic meetings.'

'But you read, you know things. You're a tutor.'

'I know some things, I . . .'

'Are there ghosts?'

Those troubled eyes frightened me.

'In books, yes. Stories.'

'Are there ghosts? Real ghosts, tell me.'

'Why do you ask?'

She looked across the field towards a pile of blackened stones on the hilltop that rose above the row of labourers' cottages near the bridge and suddenly began to walk.

'Go to hell, Johnny tutor, go to hell.'

I was due out that morning and Joanie was not. A girl down for another route had phoned in sick and it would have been easy for me to switch the schedules so we could be together but I didn't. All that afternoon as I dispensed Westerns and Mills & Boons like Valium in a half-finished housing estate I could imagine Joanie with her pile of torn covers sitting among the girls, vulnerable now to their slights, or sulking alone in the book store, gazing up at the rows of old volumes with a half-mesmerized, half-bored look.

The van got stuck in traffic and it was after six before we got back. The yard was empty with just the drivers locking up. At the corner of the lane Joanie stepped out from a boarded-up doorway and began to walk ahead of me. I had to hurry to catch her. She looked straight ahead as we walked beneath the flags along the river. We were like children, overtired and resentful.

'You lied to me,' I said.

'I was open with you, honest. You were holding back as if I couldn't give you pleasure.'

'You lied to me about your parents, about where you lived. You lied to me about who you are.'

She stopped, as if all the pent-up fury of those captive hours in the office was about to explode.

'Don't you tell me who I am. If you came from the house that I come from you'd wish you were someone else as well.'

She strode on ahead. She looked puffy, slightly ridiculous in her black lace with her shoulders stiff but her head slumped. Alone with her again, my reservations from the afternoon seemed unjust. She hurried over the bridge as I went after her.

'What has a house got to do with it? Do you think I care where you're from? You're just yourself, that's all.'

She was silent, unsure if she should be offended.

'Listen, Joanie,' I said, 'I'm sorry. Come on, I'll buy you a drink before you go home.'

That was how we wound up in bed again together. That summer the light never seemed to want to die. At a quarter to eleven there was still a grey hint of daylight, enough for me to see her face as we lay under the sheet.

'My mother died in childbirth,' Joanie whispered. 'It still happens you know. My father just died some time afterwards.'

'You don't just die.'

'In my house you do.'

She reached for the vodka beside the bed, took a slug and passed it over.

'It wasn't his house,' she said. 'Belongs to my mother's mother, my granny. She was born in the place, reared there. She'll die in the place and we'll bury her under the floorboards.'

Even as she spoke Joanie's face changed, grew more guarded, vindictive, away from me.

'He had money,' she said. 'He could have bought a house, any house. He'd the one job all his life, my Da, never missed a day sick. Do you know what my granny said when he asked to marry her daughter? "You would take away my only income, Mr Shaughnessy, you would leave me destitute."'

I reached for her hand in the bed. When I touched it she looked at me and gave a small smile as if remembering where she was.

'Never told anyone this before,' she said. 'Never understood what was happening when I was growing up. Only that my mother ran away, they might never have married at all. She had to be given away at the altar by her boss. If I ran away and got a flat I'd never go back. I'd let her rot in that stinking cottage without bothering a doctor. My granny calls it the time she was sick, but you need blood in your veins to be sick.'

Even though I held her hand, as she talked I knew from her voice that she was gone from me again, wrapped up

147

in that world. Her mother had been pregnant with Joanie when they got the letter. They had been to the bank, got the deposit for a house together. Joanie seemed to have the details of her parents' lives rehearsed in her heart, their plan to move in just for a few months until her granny was better and how those months became years when her father's wife remained somebody else's daughter. Years when a new home was always spoken of *just as soon as granny is well*.

Joanie ceased talking and shrugged her shoulders. She stretched sensually and pulled the sheet loosely around her. Her voice was suddenly expressionless.

'It's all years back now, it doesn't matter.'

'Can't be that far back,' I said, 'haven't you a baby sister?'

I could feel stiffness enter her hand like a speeded-up film of death.

'Who are you? The fucking inquisition?'

She took a slug of the vodka and put it back down on the floor. I felt cheated a second time, no longer sure what to believe about her. We stared each other out for a moment, both resentful and wary.

'Some lads get frightened if you tell them these things,' she began tentatively. 'They get the impression you're trying to land them with somebody else's mistake. Do you understand what I'm saying?'

I understood and I wanted to think it explained everything about her.

'What do you call the child?'

'Roseanna.'

'That's a nice name. Why don't we bring her out together sometime?'

'Do you mean that, mean you really don't mind?' She was excited, half sitting up in the bed with the sheet around her.

'Why should I mind?'

'Not all men would say that. You're very special and yet you don't know it.'

I was silent, giving her the chance if she wished to tell me about the father, but she had gone quiet and unsure of herself again.

'Do you like me?' she asked.

'Of course I do.'

'But how could you really?' she said. 'I've small tits and a big arse.'

'That isn't how you should see yourself.'

'But it is, isn't it? It's true, that's how people see me.'

I pulled the sheet back. She pouted, holding in her breath as if to emphasize her diminutive breasts.

'They are tiny,' she said and then rolled over, 'and I mean, just look at this.'

It was a quarter past one in the morning when I woke up after that.

'Your granny will have the National Guard out,' I said, 'and all the airports watched.'

'Let me stay,' she said sleepily and snuggled against me. 'I don't want to go back.'

It took me half an hour to persuade her to leave the bed. She kept trying, and almost succeeding, to turn my efforts into a form of foreplay. I finally had her dressed and out on the street. We got a taxi as far as the garage on top of the hill overlooking her house.

'Let me out here,' she said, 'I want to walk.' I paid the driver off and went with her, the stones of the cemetery shaded by yew trees in the moonlight on one side of the road, the bright glow of the factory skylights on the other. She paused at the bridge beside the pub and looked back.

'Think of the fun we could be having in your flat.'

'Joanie, you haven't been here for two days. If you want to leave home you should leave home, but you can't have it both ways. Come on, just put in an appearance.'

I tried to kiss her goodnight but she pulled away.

'You don't own me,' she said, 'I'm not some ornament. What are you waiting here for?'

'I want to see you go in.'

'No, you just go on now, then I'll go in.'

I turned and walked back past the mill of youths talking outside the long-closed pub, then waited a moment and returned to the corner. Joanie was walking up the hill without looking back, her eyes fixed on the new town houses with bright cars parked on the sloping driveways. Across the road on both sides of the single cottage I could see the outline of what had once been walls. She was almost past it before she slipped across the road and in the gate. There were no lights on in the cottage and none came on. I felt suddenly relieved to be rid of her and yet inexplicably alone.

I was a virgin then. Perhaps I should have mentioned that. But it still does not explain the obsession that, in the following days, seemed to border on madness. I could not wake without thinking of her. Bending down to a bored pupil I would suddenly be suffocated by an image of her. It was as if I had only to put a hand out to touch her hair, as though I could hear her breathing, the whisper of her voice. I was perpetually tense, ready to snap without reason in the schoolroom. Often in the course of reading aloud my voice would trail off as the briefest memory of that dream came back. To my horror I'd grow erect, sit at my high desk petrified somebody would enter and I'd have to stand up to greet them. My youngest pupil would stare at me inquisitively from behind her mass of curls. I'd take deep breaths, clench the book before me and try to continue.

I was due my monthly afternoon off. I walked through the wood towards her cottage, turned left up by it and took the tram into the city. Passing a pawnshop window I stared for half an hour at a row of cigarette cases before hurriedly entering to purchase one. I kept it hidden in my pockets, changing it from suit to suit as though it were stolen. I no longer ventured out on the road in search of her but spent my evenings in the Jolly Toper at a rough deal table away from the muttering locals, no longer caring that word of it could threaten my position. I was left to myself there, an outsider between classes and homes. Occasionally if I called for more drink someone at the bar might mimic my voice. They grinned in their shabby clothes, knowing they had my measure.

I'd go out and leave them to their gossip and skittles when the evening grew dark enough. I'd turn for home up past the Protestant church, waiting till I was alone before cutting across the fields towards the wood. The rich lunatics were cloistered in high rooms out of sight behind the ordered trees and shrubs I could glimpse through Farnham's Gates. I'd cross Savages Lane and listen, always convinced I could hear an old man's footsteps dogging my own. Below on the road the light of a cart might pass.

I'd keep well back among oak and yew trees, ragwort and day lilies. Field wood rush, *quinach leana* in my mother's tongue, *luzula campestris* in Hegerty's. I had the words for everything except what I was searching for. The stuttering child of poverty, the orphan, the classical scholarship boy, the tutor with a pressed handkerchief in his breast pocket. I was none of them any longer. I was only a man with passion, with lust. My behaviour was madness but the things Hegerty had craved for me no longer made sense. The room with a brass bed and the maid who brought water. A place above the footman who could look down on the gardener. Even his cold perfection of Latin seemed as empty as my father's roofless hovel in Sligo.

By the gates of the lower madhouse at the bridge I would hear my blood pumping so loudly that it drowned out whatever inexplicable screams came from behind the high walls. I would think of starved uncles and aunts as I stared at the overgrown famine mound across the road, of names my father had kept alive, names that died in his final breath of cholera. I'd cross the stream where cattle shied away in the darkness and wait where I could see the lights of the cottages. Above at Cross Guns her father would be working in the mill, his face whitened by dust like a spectre's. It was on the third night that I saw Bridget emerge through the back window. She glanced behind her in terror as though looking at someone, then turned and plunged down the grassy slope towards the stream. I drew myself into the shadows, frightened of being seen by her. She wore a long linen nightdress and had a rough blanket around her shoulders that spread out like a cloak as she raced into the trees. My heart thumped and I was soaked in sweat. Had she guessed at my nightly vigil, was she somehow offering herself? Or was there somebody in her room who had been terrorizing her? I glanced towards the open window waiting for a body to appear. Bridget had vanished up the steep wooded slope behind the small dairy. I approached the cottage cautiously. The rooms were in darkness. I crept to the open window and knelt down. There was a small bed in the corner with the clothes thrown back. A bluebottle that had bumbled its way in was bashing itself against the glass. Its buzzing grated on my nerves. I wanted to enter but was too scared. I glanced behind and reached one hand in. It touched a piece of cloth on the floor. I drew it out and found I was holding a petticoat. I pressed my face against its cool folds, closed my eyes in a white bliss and breathed in the scent of her. A door opened in a neighbouring cottage, a man letting out a dog who began to bark. I dropped the petticoat back inside and, reaching into my pocket to take out the gold cigarette case, let it fall on to the cloth on the floor with a muted thud. The dog was jumping at the stone wall between the gardens. 'Rabbits,' the man said, cursing him, and closed the door. I turned and as I ran back down the slope I thought how someone watching would think that it was I who was the chasing figure Bridget had run in terror from.

After that I found myself drinking with Joanie most evenings, going to bed before closing time, having to struggle later on to get her home. One or two mornings a week a phone call would come in to work that she was sick, but I knew I'd find her in a doorway down the lane when I left the yard. For six weeks it lasted, awkward breaks in work sitting at different tables from each other in the scabby canteen, drunken pay-day nights when we would be flush with cash, other evenings when I had barely food in the flat. I liked that about her, how she didn't care when money was tight. We'd just take to the bed earlier, walk out past the cemetery after midnight to her house.

Her dreams were simple, a flat anywhere near town, trips down to the Red Corner furniture shop to fit it out with cheap mock antiques. Heavy curtains and a dim red bulb in the corner. She kept that room in her mind, brought it out in a softer voice when we were alone in bed, changing the furnishings around, the colour of the carpet, describing some table she had seen in a window.

'And an old-fashioned wooden cot in the corner,' I whispered once and then regretted speaking. What landlord in Dublin would want to know a single mother with a child? If she left home we both knew what would await her, the ninth floor of a Ballymun tower block or a house out in the foothills of Tallaght.

'Bring the child out,' I said. 'Saturday. We'll take her up to the Phoenix Park.'

She smiled and nodded her head on the pillow but I knew by then that on Saturday she would arrive by herself. Her excitement at my acceptance of the child was gone. She had never mentioned her again, as if no connection was allowed between her life with me and the world of that house. I had never glimpsed her granny or her child. All I had ever seen was her sister running for videos at night and the light that never seemed to go out when I lingered in the shadows of the old wall on the hill, not wanting to go back alone to the flat with its crumpled bed still warm from our flesh, not wanting to lose the curious tacky magic which remained with me after she had left.

It was two weeks after we met that a youth passed us one night at the traffic lights. He was around twenty, with that puffed up, glazed look which comes from medication. Joanie stared after him.

'That's the creep who found the room where the girl was locked up,' she said. 'Johnny Whelan. Lives with his granny up the North Road. The fellow's been a spacer ever since.'

I had no idea what she was talking about. Joanie pointed up at the last of the old Corporation houses on the hilltop overlooking the cemetery.

'You see the house at the end of the street where the light is still burning,' she said, 'that's in the room where the girl was locked up. You remember, it was in all the papers about three years ago?'

I did remember now. The photographs of the room came back. It felt eerie standing among the crowds spilling out from the pub with nobody even bothering to glance up at it.

'You mean someone lives there now?'

'It's been bought from the Corporation and done up and sold again. Why wouldn't someone live there? Worse things have happened. Used to play nicknacks on her when I was growing up and she'd chase us down the road with a black knife. There were stories about her but it was just like the films, you didn't have to believe them when the lights came back on.'

'But is it a family living there now?'

'How would I know?' She shrugged her shoulders. 'I don't go near that house. Who cares anyway?'

I crossed into a small park by the stream while Joanie lagged behind, upset at my interest. I could discern the outline of a row of toys and the poster of a pop star in the window.

'How can children sleep there?' I asked. 'In that same room?'

'Why the hell shouldn't they?' Joanie almost shouted. 'The past is the past, you're the guy who is always saying that. No connections, no ties, eh. Well, it's their house now, they can do what they like in it.'

I looked around. Joanie was sulking, yet I knew it was more than just her usual quickly forgotten tantrum. She was genuinely upset about something.

'What's wrong?' I asked gently.

She shrugged her shoulders.

'It's done enough damage that house. I should never have shown it to you. Gives me the creeps up there.'

'Were you ever in it?'

For a moment I didn't think she was going to answer.

'I knew someone who was.'

The almost angry abandonment she normally possessed was gone. It was like she was deflated, like somebody had let the air out of her. I smiled to try and cheer her.

'Is this the girl who watches horror videos every night?'

'It's all right in films, it's sick in real life.'

The next morning in the house Bridget looked distraught and haggard. I glimpsed her down a corridor kneeling beside a cast-iron bucket. She leaned back on her knees holding the floor cloth in one hand as she wiped the back of her wrist across her brow. She lowered her hand and noticed me watching her. Her eyes were glazed, terror filled. She rinsed the cloth in the bucket and stretched her shoulders forward, scrubbing the cold marble without once looking back up. I climbed the stairs and leaned out across the banisters to gaze down at her, her body thrusting forward with the cloth, the outline of her buttocks through the uniform jutting higher than her head. What did I feel? A sense of unexplained power. Whatever secret she carried she carried alone. I was suddenly dizzy, that boy again running around the Black Church to meet the devil. I thought I had missed him but he had been inside me all along, waiting to envelop my limbs. I wanted Bridget, I wanted her fear, the smell of sweat and other moistures I had never known. My knuckles were white on the banisters, my legs trembled. She straightened her shoulders and arched her neck back, her eyes rising up to stare straight at mine. She never flinched from my gaze. It was I who drew back and stumbled down the corridor, still seeing her in my mind, arched there like a swan, as motionless as some obscene Chinese statuette.

Was she scared and needing help or trying to snare me in some trap? Below the windows of my room the rich got on with their jaded, pathetic lives; carriages drawing up, a gentleman and lady on horseback, the dull thud of croquet in the distance like skulls being cracked open. I snapped more violently at my pupils, not caring what they reported back. The little girl was near tears, her fingers, trained for a life of ringing bells, dug so tightly into her arm that they left slender red impressions on her skin.

I lay in my room till evening. The pillow might have been a rock under my neck. I twisted and tried to reason with myself but I was in the grip of something that was no longer rational. I heard the voices of maids leaving by the back door. I could imagine her running through the woods, knew she would be waiting at that gap in the hedgerow. Just when it seemed I had won I began to shiver as though I would die if I stayed there. I pulled the door open and ran through the corridor. I told myself I just had to escape into the air to clear my head but I knew where my hurrying boots were going.

I watched her through the trees anxiously entwining her hands, turning her face away when a carriage or a man passed on the road. She stared across the low meadow towards the smoke of the cottages and did not look at me directly when I found the courage to climb down and join her.

'Were you here last night?' she demanded. 'You must tell me, I must know.'

'Why do you think I was here?'

Bridget produced a white cloth and unwrapped the cigarette case. It looked cheap and battered in the dull evening light.

'I told no other man, no living soul about my dream, my joke. My father will be due home from the village. He must leave again for work in the mill soon. He'll beat me in the morning if I should miss him. Tell me, Sir, be honest I beg you, is this yours?'

I nodded in guilt.

'Thanks be to the Lord, thank you, Sir.' She pushed it quickly back into my hands. 'Now take it back before someone finds it.'

'If you had told nobody then who else could it belong to? Are you in trouble, girl? Last night I saw you run from your room as if being pursued. Is it a man from the village threatening you?'

She shook her head violently.

'Not a man, no . . .'

She stopped, hearing footsteps at the bend. Whoever was approaching was whistling 'The Blackbird'. Bridget suddenly sprang forward, tearing her clothes and skin on the briars as she tumbled down the gully into the field. Her fear was contagious. I put the cigarette case in my pocket, swung my foot forward and leapt before he came into sight. I slid down, winding myself as I banged against rocks before she caught me as my feet were about to strike the water. We huddled beneath the bushes there, our bodies packed together, our breath close until the man had passed.

'My father,' she whispered. 'If I run across the meadow I'll be there before him. Let me go now, Sir, or I shall be late.'

She was trembling as I held my arm around her. I knew she would not pull away.

'Don't you know the danger of running around in the

dark like that? When I saw you last night you seemed like a wild thing.'

'I'll not sleep there alone, Sir, not in that house. He leaves me there till dawn with not a soul else.'

'There are neighbours on both sides of you. Can you not call out if you are in distress?'

'And tell them what, Sir?' Bridget turned towards me. 'What will I tell them I see?'

There was something about her voice, a violence below the surface which unnerved me. Which of us was the other's prisoner in that glade? Had she tumbled down there to escape her father or lure me after her? She was waiting for a reply, her eyes defying me to speak.

'How can I know what you could tell them? I have never been in your room at night.'

'My father takes a lift home from the cart bringing the first load of flour to Drogheda each morning. It leaves at seven, has him at the bridge by a quarter past.'

'That is a long time from sundown.'

'The man who visits my room, tutor, will not leave until dawn or until I tell him to go. Do you understand?'

It made sense to me suddenly, her counterfeit mysterious airs like a melodrama heroine, her running across the meadow in her night shift, this enticement beside the stream where we might be seen from the roadway. What was she but a labourer's daughter without a dowry or education? What future could await her in this village or the city in the vale beneath it? Lying under the rough trunk of some farm labourer, a cabin of screeching children, her looks dissipated by the age of twenty-four? Her look of terror was the bait and I the dumb fish swimming towards it. The slight position I held in the world, the few possessions I had so recently despised all came back to me, suddenly precious at the thought that I might lose them. She rose up as though reading my thoughts.

'I want nothing from you, especially a child. Do you hear me?'

She began to race frantically across the grass towards her father's cottage, her words, as she shouted back, distorted by the wind so I could barely believe I had deciphered them, that they came from her lips and were not an echo of my dream.

'Get me pregnant, Johnny tutor, and I'll claw your balls off.'

The mood of the office had changed. At first it was just cigarettes, then change began to disappear, then banknotes from people's purses and coats. An air of suspicion set in, destroying the ease of that summer, girls brought their bags with them to the toilets, people put their cigarettes away without passing them around. Library assistants always blame the cleaners. It's a form of tribal snobbery, I suppose. No doubt the cleaners always blame them. Joanie suffered the greatest loss. She emerged from the cloak-room in tears one pay-day saying that her wages were stolen. The girls quietly had a whip-round and forced an envelope into her pocket when she was leaving at five o'clock.

We blew it all that night in half a dozen pubs, could barely stand when we reached my flat. In bed, for some reason, I told her about my father's mother who had died when I was nine. I remembered her as a great woman to walk, even in her late seventies, remembered one Sunday how she had brought me around the whole Botanic Gardens and then to the corner outside to buy ice-cream.

'Slut's Alley,' she'd said, pointing down the road bordering the river, 'that's what they called it when I was a girl in the fields out there.'

I lay with my head against Joanie's breast, trying to remember more. Had she shown me a small house where she had lived, a hill, something to do with horses and a tram? All I remembered was the ice-cream, a sliver of cone stuck between my teeth as she told me I was the spit of her father, and wondering if I asked her would she buy me a second one.

'Your granny might have known her,' I said to Joanie. 'You could ask, but I can't remember her maiden name.'

Joanie was silent, I wasn't even sure if she was listening. It was only after I had almost forgotten what I had said that she replied.

'I'll not ask her. I'll not be in that woman's debt for anything.'

But yet often in midweek when we were at our most broke Joanie would arrive with money borrowed from the old woman. No pay-night could match the unexpected joy of those sprees, the doubles bought, the full bottle at closing time, her persistent moaning during sex. And never would I have to fight harder to persuade her to go home and to persuade myself to make her go before this room wound up her special flat.

Because deep down I knew that our being together was a spree and had to be kept at that, a defiant fling against the world by a girl embarking on womanhood and a man leaving his youth behind. Left alone here to cope with the mundane tasks of living we would quarrel before long, retreat into sulks, tear each other apart. And yet by then I wanted it to be more and felt that she did too, but Joanie was frightened of any show of affection that went too close. Her favourite phrase was that she was my mistress, letting the word hang in the air as though it belonged to another century, that we were drawn together by sex and nothing else. She hated any term of affection. Brittle and bright in her white stockings and tops she held me for that moment only, her cries echoing through the empty showrooms below my flat, down the crumbling stairways as she came repeatedly on her back. Sometimes afterwards, if her pleasure had been too great, she would not let me kiss her. She'd talk of other men she'd had, either real or imagined, her voice shriller than necessary as if to drive her emotions back. Did she love me? That is the question I still keep asking myself. Perhaps in as much as she allowed herself to love anything. I told myself that it was the child which held her back, that she kept for her daughter alone a space in her heart. I know even less now than I knew then, not even if I loved her in return. She could annoy me intensely with her attempts at ostentation, her shame at the cottage she was born in, her dreams of mock Victoriana tacked on to the bricks of some new estate, her flight from everything that both she and I were made of. And yet I kept thinking that I still didn't know her, that there was a different Joanie living in the secret world of that cottage, that there was something I was missing, something that was strangely familiar, some part of her I was failing to decipher.

Once I gave in. It was my thirty-first birthday but I had not told Joanie so. Indeed, I had forgotten myself until I looked at a paper that morning. In bed that night she was staring at my face. I suddenly realized how old I must look to her, how many years had passed since those mornings when I had run through the fields, feeling the future open before me. When had it gone stale, like a summer you've kept waiting for before realizing the leaves have crinkled up into autumn? That childish sense of destiny had somehow sustained me, made me oblivious to how my youth had slid away. Joanie smiled, noticing my seriousness. I didn't want her ever to leave, to have to pass those last hours of every night alone, the grey light on the quays when I could not sleep, the red glow of a cigarette growing less and less discernible through the window.

'Stay with me, Joanie,' I said. 'Not just for this night but every night. Bring your child. I don't mean here but some house we could rent. It could be good, just the three of us, no one looking over our shoulders.'

'I'll stay tonight if you want,' she said. 'You know that's no problem.'

'Joanie, I want you to come and live with me. Do you not understand? You hate that cottage, I virtually have to kill to get you to go back to it. Let's start together, I honestly don't mind about the child.'

She rolled over on her back and was silent. I had wanted her voice to be ecstatic, her arms to be flung around me.

'Just like that, and leave her?' Joanie's voice was doubtful.

'Leave who? I want you to bring the child with you.'

'Leave my granny?'

I laughed and then stopped, seeing her face.

'But you hate her? You spend half the night thinking up plans to poison her off.'

'She'd like that, wouldn't she, the shame of me packed away off her hands. She'd think she'd have won a victory for herself.'

Her voice was flat and vindictive. I'm too old, I told myself at first. That is what she is thinking, but she doesn't know how to say it to me. And then I sensed that she was hardly even aware of me, that her thoughts were firmly back in that cottage, in her other world I was excluded from.

'Joanie, I'm not discussing your granny, I'm talking about the future, about us, you and me and your child. What is it? Is it leaving your sister you're worried about? We could find a way for her too.'

'Sitting snug up there alone with those cosy rooms finally to herself. Oh, my granny would have the last laugh to herself all right.'

Joanie sat up in the bed. Her hands were folded across her stomach and she was half rocking herself. That night I didn't have to force her to dress. We walked the mile and a half out to her home in silence. At the corner she never acknowledged me or looked back. She walked up the hill, this time ignoring the town houses and bright cars, her eyes fixed on the dark windows of her granny's cottage as though it were an heirloom some thief had tried to wrestle from her.

The first thing to do was try and appear calm for the rest of the evening, be seen about the house, complain of a headache and go to my room. The next thing was to wait, counting each chime, like a slow torture, from the clock in the hall. The last thing was to leave the house quietly. The back stairs were in semi-darkness. Only a single oil lamp near the bust of the Italian girl shone its weak light out in a dim circle. I crept past it and down, out the side door across the back lawn towards the woods. Some fields were to be crossed, the overgrown ramparts which a Dutch king, now snug in his crypt in Delft, had dug with his battle-tired men, and then I was safe among the foliage.

At worst now I might be mistaken for a poacher. I kept

close to the river, crossing it once by two planks strung across the water, one for my hands three feet above the other. It was a quarter moon, just bright enough to discern the rough track through the trees. I left the sound of water and ventured deeper through the old woods. None of the serving girls would walk this way at night, though it saved half an hour on their journey down the avenue of stiff regimented boughs. Many had died here of hunger and smallpox, but it was not the ghosts of their own class who frightened the girls but a past master, a hanging judge said to ride here by night, his name more real to them, a century after the last worm had crawled from his bones, than the place names of Boston or India.

I did not meet him that night. Two startled rabbits crossed my path, a badger raised his head and sniffed, slipping into the undergrowth, and once I heard footsteps which ceased when I did. As I walked on I knew I was being observed by no spectre but by old Matthew, a crouched figure of blood and flesh and hunger. I would have been frightened of being seen by anyone else but he seemed no more than an animal in the wood. I felt the cigarette case in my pocket and stopped, emptying the contents out on to the clay track. I threw matches down and walked on, listening to the eager footsteps shuffling out from behind the trees.

I came to the wood's edge near the ruins of a burnt-out cotton mill where disturbed rooks circled with rasping cries, slipped past the lights of a cabin and paused by the barred gates of the asylum. Nobody screamed from behind the walls that night, instead from the gatekeeper's cottage a child sang a song without words.

I crossed the road, then froze at the hedgerow. The boy, Turlough, was there, looking around him lost as he tried to find his way home. I waited till he was past before plunging down the slope to leap across the stream. Up till now I had not allowed myself to think of what lay ahead. Instead, I had focused on every bird's late cry and creature's blind haste, never so aware of every leaf and burrow hole as I tried to obliterate the thoughts of it from my head.

But now the time for control was gone. I thought only of Bridget. I forgot dowry and doubts and the ordered universe of walls. I was an animal stalking through the undergrowth and she was my prey. There was no longer any part of her body my mind could not conjure, no part I would not make my own. I crouched down crossing the meadow, and approached the cottage from the rear. The kitchen window was small, set deep into the wall. I watched her through it. Her hair was still damp from washing, she knelt with her head bowed over the fire to dry it as though she were at prayer. The room was spotless, with little furniture. Over the fireplace a large cross hung, the crumpled body of her Saviour suspended between nails. On another wall the cross of her namesake was nailed over the door. I rapped three times on the glass and she turned her head sharply and then stopped, her face concealed by the fan of hair. It was only when I rapped again that she rose, struggled to make out my face in the window, and then ran to push open the back door.

'It's you, Sir,' she said.

'Let me in, girl, quickly before somebody sees us.'

She remained blocking the door.

'You'll stay until I tell you to go? You will?'

'Quickly, Bridget, let me in.'

'Promise first.'

I promised and she stepped back, closing the door behind me as I entered.

'Till just before dawn,' she whispered, almost to herself.

'You may wish yourself well rid of me before then for all you know of what I may do.'

'What you do is of little consequence,' she murmured, 'just be here and watch.' She paused for a moment near the table. 'And don't leave me your bastard to carry in my father's name.'

Once I had been at the heart of everything in work. Now I was not told about the trap that was set, the marked five-pound note left in a girl's locker. It was an August afternoon when the heat in that cramped room was at its most oppressive. Joanie had just returned from the ladies when the Senior Assistant came in. There was a hush that was louder than any whisper along the table. He nervously cleared his throat.

'We all know that money has been going missing,' he said. 'Now I'm asking everyone at the table to empty their pockets and purses. I'm not forcing people but if anyone does not agree I shall have to call the police in.'

Billy lowered his paper and looked over at me. I knew what he was thinking, how the fun of that summer had drained from the office, the laughter and trust, the 'spurious camaraderie' our bosses had complained of. Each of us felt like a criminal as we emptied our pockets, embarrassed for no reason at the trivial personal possessions on display. Joanie scattered the contents of her bag on the table, a large assortment of different types of cigarettes and a few crumpled notes. The Senior Assistant picked up a five-pound note from among them. The letters I.L.Y.A. were written clearly across it, the first and second pairs of letters in different hands.

'Are they your initials and did you write them?' he asked the two girls nearest him. They nodded. Joanie looked coldly in his face.

'What are you talking about? He gave that to me after our first night together.' She pointed across at me. 'I.L.Y.A. I love you always. I've kept this in my purse ever since.'

'In two different letterings?'

'I.L. with his right hand, Y.A. with his left. To show that he loved me with both his body and his mind.'

Nobody believed her. The room looked on as Joanie stared at my face. The Senior Assistant walked awkwardly towards me. He was one of my best friends, a man I could trust with my soul. He didn't want to ask me and I didn't want to answer him. I felt violated as if my whole world had been inexplicably snatched away.

'Is that true?'

I nodded and lowered my head. He gave the note back to Joanie and walked towards the door.

'Don't I get an apology?' she demanded.

He stopped and looked back at the contents of her bag.

'You've varied tastes in cigarettes,' he said.

Joanie looked him up and down contemptuously.

'I've better taste in men.'

At five o'clock I went into the gents and remained there until I was sure she would have left the yard, then took my coat and walked out. But I knew I was only stalling the moment. She was waiting outside my flat.

'The bitches, they set me up, the jealous bitches.'

The shopkeeper was piling up his couches in the hall, sodden with drizzle, up-ended to reveal the bad lining and cheap wood. I walked past him, ignoring her, and she followed me to the bend of the stairs.

'You don't believe them, do you? You would take their side against mine.'

'*I love you always*. What would you have replied if I had said that to you?' I had the key in the lock, the words spoken to the badly painted door.

'You never did say that, did you?' She paused. What did I expect? Her hand suddenly to be on my shoulder, her voice to ask forgiveness?

'Anything I stole I stole for you, I spent on you. Did you

see me with a scrap of new clothes, did you ever know about all the evenings I walked here so I could even spend the bus fare on you?'

I heard her footsteps descend. I put my hand on the door. Instead of painted wood, for a moment I imagined her skin slightly glistening after we had made up, had found an excuse to carry on. And I knew that, even as I had waited in the gents and cursed her walking along the quays, part of me had already been anticipating our reunion in the bed. When I reached the window she was walking across the bridge, her shoulders straight as if she knew she was being watched, her brown hair, the way I loved it, waving back.

Bridget's bedroom was plain. A small window was set deeply in the wall, the wooden lattice spilling its shadow like a crucifix across the stone flags. I paused awkwardly beside the bed and tried to kiss her but she pulled away.

'Why did you ask me here?' I said.

She shrugged her shoulders. Her eyes had lost that unease. They seemed cold as though staring at something beyond me. She gave the same smile I had only seen hinted at before. I put my hands on her shoulders and she sat on the white linen bedspread. When I began to undress her, she shrugged my hands crossly away.

'I can do that myself,' she snapped and, keeping her eyes on my face, began to unbutton her dress. She was naked when she lifted the blanket to climb in and turned on her side as though oblivious to my presence and ready to sink into a long-awaited sleep. Nervously I undressed. Her behaviour was erratic, I was not sure what she would do next. When I climbed in beside her would she feign sleep or scream for the neighbours? Would I be trapped here by men with pitchforks and sticks while she sobbed innocently in the corner? She had left an oil lamp on the small stool beside the bed. I debated whether or not to extinguish it. I wished to see her naked and yet felt I would have more courage in the darkness. I quenched the lamp. That night would compensate for the hundreds spent alone in Shallon House, for the thousands of slights to remind me of my place. Now I wanted her and all I could feel was my want. There was nothing I would not have promised for her to let me join her in that bed and, I realized with a chill, nothing I would not do to keep her there till I was finished, no matter how hard she might plead to escape.

I lifted the rough blanket and climbed in. It was cool beneath me. I lay still, staring at the whitewashed ceiling while I sensed the warmth emanating from her skin a few bare inches from my side. My penis had grown hard and suddenly I wanted it over, now while the strength was in me. I felt a terror that I would stall, grow limp before I had even touched her flesh. Again, as in that dream, I felt as if I had stepped outside this time and world. Had I seduced her, had she led me here or was there something else which neither of us could control, a devious god, a retarded creator playing games with us? What was she thinking as she lay there, what did she expect of me?

Every inch of me yearned to roll into her warmth. It was like clinging to the edge of a slope, knowing you were about to fall, and as I turned I could sense her fear, filling the entire room, an overwhelming aura of apprehension. I expected her to push me away but instead she clung to me in a sort of desperate yielding. Her skin was damp, I could feel the beads of sweat beneath my hands. We never spoke, mouth just tearing against mouth, flesh rubbing against flesh, two panting breaths punctuating the silence, two bodies uncertain of where to go next. Twice I tried to enter her and she quickly moved her thighs to dislodge me. Then her hands moved down my flat stomach and she began to massage my penis as though milking a young cow. She lay astride me, her tongue alive and wet in my throat, her other arm stretched across my chest to hinder my hands and her thighs locked against mine as I tried to writhe from her grip. She was stronger than I could have imagined and it would have needed physical violence to dislodge her. I lay back then as the pleasure increased and let her have her way. She loosened her grip as she felt my resistance weaken and half sat over me, her mouth still in mine but her hand now pressed against the pillow to keep her torso arced. I could feel it coming now and knew she could too from the tremors of my body. Her mouth plunged deeper into mine, her teeth nipped cruelly against my tongue when I twisted my head away in shock as the spasms racked my body which she was holding down.

Her breasts were smeared and the underside of her neck.

I could feel the sperm lying on my face, knew the pillow and the wall behind me were speckled. Bridget was gazing down at her body as though astonished to find the white substance there. Her forcefulness had vanished, she was timid, anxious again as she covered her breasts with the sheet.

'You will stay till dawn now, won't you?' she whispered.

If I answered I do not remember it. Her fear was needless. Even if I had wished to I doubt if I could have risen. The drowsy after-taste of sex had spread to every part of my body, filling it with sleep like a warm tide washing in to obliterate everything. That's the last I remember, her blurred face peering down and the stains from her breasts already beginning to come through the white sheet she was clutching against her flesh.

A week passed when the only sign of Joanie was a sick cert sent in by post. There were whispers in the vans that ceased when I entered. The others would cluster around me as I worked, awkwardly trying to show their friendship. On the following Thursday the girl sent for the wages was told that Joanie had called in earlier to collect her own for herself.

There was a talent contest on that night. Sharon, a new girl in work, was singing. I loathed such events but joined the few girls who wandered out to watch her. I needed to feel part of something, even though I knew the same ease I had felt among them would never be there again. Besides, I couldn't bear another night alone with just the unsold furniture in the hallway of my flat. The pub was at the top of the old main street up from the carriageway near Joanie's house. Red leather seats wrapped themselves into alcoves where clusters of supporters for each act were gathered. The amplification was terrible but it didn't really matter. Whoever had persuaded the most friends to pay into the half-full lounge and vote for them would win at the end of the night.

We drank with our back to the stage, shouting over the static from the speakers. There are times when I drink for pleasure, and times I just drink. That was one of those nights; a rich melancholy void had settled within me. I was older than anyone else at the table except Billy. I had wasted a decade working on those throbbing blue trucks with nothing except a shabby flat littered with books and a hundred and fifty record albums. Sometimes old schoolmates beeped at me in their cars, business suits and mortgages, the comfortable monotony of family cares. They looked so aged they frightened me away from the mirror.

I knew that in a suit I would look even older than them. Yet at that table with the thump of poxy music in the air, it seemed I could remain suspended for as long as I drank, a solitary age that was neither young nor old. Most of the girls were drifting off for buses. I knew I should too but I hung on to the end. Sharon climbed back down to join us, flushed and slightly embarrassed from the thrill of singing to the backing tape, but knowing she had not won. I wished I could have bought fifty admission tickets without her knowing and sent her home with that trashy silver cup. The MC was announcing the winner to screams from a far corner. The two girls left consoled Sharon. Apart from them, just Billy and I remained in front of a mass of slops in stacked glasses.

I knew why I was waiting there, though I had not admitted it to myself. I was not surprised or happy or sad when Joanie appeared, I just felt that the spell of drink was broken and I was suddenly locked back into my own age. She was wearing a duffle coat that was too large for her. It looked incongruous with the black dress she wore underneath. Some locals nodded to her. Two youths at a table laughed and muttered something when she passed.

Although the bar had closed she went up and they served her. When she came down it seemed like she had bought drinks for everyone. She pushed a double vodka across to Billy who shook his head to refuse it and another to me, then took the other four vodkas on the tray and emptied them into a tall glass in front of her. I knew how hard it was for her to sit beside the girls who ignored her, yet I gave her no help, sitting back with Billy and letting her suffer. After a few moments Billy leaned across to clink his untouched glass against hers, then placed it down, smiled sadly and departed.

The girls left shortly afterwards. Joanie and I had still not spoken. I downed my glass, took my jacket and walked outside. She followed suit. We stood together at the foot of a huge metal bridge. I could smell vinegar from the chip shop behind us. I felt cold and pure and empty. The coat made her shapeless, her bowed head indistinct in the darkness. She looked suddenly as young as she really was. I felt sorry for something in her that I knew I could not comprehend.

'You should go home, Joanie,' I said, 'it's late.'

She shook her head.

'Not going back alone to that bloody cottage.'

'Where will you sleep then?' I asked, then paused. 'If you won't go home you can have the bed in my gaff and I'll sleep on the floor. Just for this night, give you a start. You should make the break away from that house.'

Joanie shook her head and looked up.

'A real man wouldn't have just left me like that. If you were a real man you'd punish me like a Victorian would his mistress.'

I gazed at her, yet there was no trace of mockery on that solemn face or in her voice.

'I'm not some Victorian. Go on home, Joanie. I'm tired of all these games.'

'If you were a real man you'd sleep with me tonight, sleep in my room.'

'And what about your granny?'

'My granny is deaf. She won't hear us no matter what things you did to me.'

How long I slept I have no real idea. That part of the night seemed to pass in an entangled succession of sleeping and waking nightmares. Even now I am unsure how much of it I dreamt and how much I experienced. All I remember is waking that first time to find Bridget hunched up in the bed with her eyes fixed on one corner of the room, then trawling slowly along the wall as though tracing a movement. I could feel an incomprehensible dread within me and I knew it was that fear which had woken me rather than her shifting in the bed.

'Can you feel her? Can you, tutor? She's still here. I thought with somebody else here she wouldn't dare to come, but there she is. Can you see her? Can you?'

The room seemed the same as before I had slept, although a little more distinct with my eyes now adjusted to the dark. Moonlight slid in through a slight gap in the curtain. Everything was in its place, the only thing strange was the girl herself, hunched up into the smallest possible space, unable to lift her eyes from what she saw or imagined she saw around her. I reached out my hand and placed it on her shoulder to comfort her. She turned with wild eyes towards me.

'Are you blind, tutor? Are you taunting me? There, look in front of you!'

'Calm yourself, Bridget,' I said. 'There is nothing here except the pair of us. It is just a nightmare you're after having. I assure you there is nothing.'

Bridget's eyes returned to where they had been staring and repeated the last word coldly with a resigned air. She looked down at me again and laughed bitterly to herself.

'Then it was for nothing I allowed you in here to use me. For nothing.'

She drew the sheet more closely about her body and resumed watching whatever phantom she imagined was there. It is hard to describe lying in the cold after-shock of sex which had not really taken place at all, beside a woman who did not want me. Walking through the woodlands it was I who had seen myself as the hunter drawing his net gradually in. Now I realized it was Bridget who had tolerated my interest and allowed me to fall into her scheme. She had regarded me with such contempt as to have confidence in manipulating even the sexual act so that instead of the conquest I had dreamt of my seed mocked me in dry stains on the sheet.

And then I thought of the terror which must have lain behind her actions. To lead on a man into her very bed, to risk everything sooner than face a night alone there by herself. The scene unnerved me, the crouched figure whose terrified eyes moved slowly as if witnessing some act. Her very weakness gave me strength. I rose from the bed and reached for my clothes. It took Bridget a moment to realize what was happening. Then she sprang forward and ran towards me.

'You promised!' she shouted. 'You promised.'

I motioned her out of my way and she blocked the door with her body.

'Go back and watch,' she said like a trapped animal. 'If you look long enough you will see her. You must, I can't be mad. Try to leave now, tutor, and I swear I will kill you. Do you hear me, tutor?'

The girl was deranged, I decided, and it had been crazy of me to even think of going there. There were brothels on every second corner of Dublin. Why had I been so crazy as to risk my job, my position for this one failed night? I knew I had to get away as soon as possible. How could I be sure her father might not return, that the hours she gave me for him were not invented? I grabbed her wrist and pushed her from the door so fiercely that she sprawled on the floor behind me, and I had the lock turned before I felt the searing pain in the base of my skull. She had struck me with a poker which had hung in the unlit fireplace. I half fell to my knees, clutching my head and as I turned I saw her frightened eyes staring at me. She backed away as I rose and I followed her until she stopped against the side of the bed. It took one slap to send her across it. I looked at my hand in astonishment. I had never struck anybody in my life, never known myself capable of such an act. I stared at her cheek which was already turning red and she made a choking sound that I thought was a cry. Instead she laughed, long and high as if the noise came from deeper within her than her normal voice. The sheet she was wrapped in was undone.

'Get me pregnant and I'll kill you, Johnny Johnny,' she repeated twice. She said she was a virgin. She only cried out once. This time I had no fear of failure. When my time came I withdrew and with my own hand covered her stomach and breasts again with glistening white pearls. As I lay, drifting once more towards sleep, I asked had it been too sore, had she known any pleasure. Her voice was drowsy also, distant as though coming from somewhere else.

'I think she is pleased, tutor.'

'What are you saying, girl?'

I remember trying to wake up, puzzled by her words.

'I think she is pleased with the Johnny Johnny I've brought her.'

Why did I go back with her? It was like I was no longer just myself, something was stirring within me, some illicit thrill I was too drunk to fight that seemed both foreign and familiar, as if I had felt it once before so long ago that I could not fully remember. I let Joanie lead the way with part of my mind clicked off. I realized how she had deliberately tried to make me feel superior in the words she had chosen, in subjecting herself to such a public reunion. It was as if she had created roles for the pair of us, outdated roles I did not wish for, and yet I could not even be sure if she was aware of her manipulation.

She was quiet now as we walked in the glare of headlights down the carriageway. When we reached the railings of the old dairy she stopped, then suddenly began to climb up over them. She beckoned me to follow. I shrugged my shoulders and jumped up.

A night-watchman smoked in a raised wooden hut near the entrance gate, his eyes not seeing the empty milk trucks and stacked crates in front of him. His face looked waxen and yellow in the security lights. Joanie ran across the tarmacadam to the side of the building and scrambled up the far wall into the shadows of the hillside. The lights were on in the building. I could hear the cleaners' voices as I climbed up, searching for her. I felt uneasy suddenly, a quiet terror. I shook my head, imagined her lips suddenly tasting of vodka and sin. How long was it since I had used that word? A tree was growing sideways from the cliff-edge of wasteland that towered over the dairy. I reached the crest and found her resting against the trunk.

Sin. I remembered when there was something to sin against. A child in my local church where the late winter sun blunted the light in the stained-glass panes into faded blobs like cancer on a lung in an X-ray or a mark on my soul. I followed Joanie's gaze beyond the cluster of floodlit buildings. Below us a little stream trickled out from a concrete pipe and meandered through the darkness towards the bridge. The carriageway was smooth and blue like a model in a shop window at Christmas. I had been happy back then, something to sin against, a right and a wrong. I thought of my schoolmates again, the lower ranks of party members, residents' association chairmen, studying for late degrees in public administration. *Sin.* When the first illusion died I could believe in no other. On the hill beyond I could see an estate of houses and the squat roofs of the industrial estate and I realized that, below them, Joanie was staring at the caved-in rafters and bricked-up windows of an old gate-lodge beside the traffic lights. I remembered one night trying not to smile when she claimed it had once been the entrance to the residence of her grandmother's mother.

'The family residence before you fell on hard times,' I joked. 'If she came back now she'd think you were living in the servants' quarters.'

It was windy up on the headland. Joanie's hair blew about her face as she stared at me.

'That was an asylum, didn't you know? They locked her up when she was young.'

A container lorry moved off from the lights, changing gears as it faced up the hill towards the north. Joanie raised her face so I could see how the moonlight softened it.

'I look the image of her. That's what my granny always told me when I was young.'

I could see it too, although I had never seen a photograph of the woman. But in that moonlight Joanie's features were like an old black and white print. The duffle coat was open and her cheap black dress and her hair, even the arc of her neck as she leaned her head back, all seemed from another century. Was it my imagination or was she suddenly scared to be out there, isolated on that last untouched headland away from the comforting lights of the suburb?

'When did she go mad?' I asked, realizing that my voice was apologetic.

'She gave birth to my granny in there. It was a scandal. Her father lost his job in some local mill for refusing to give the child up.'

'Was it the same house you lived in?'

'Yes, but only the back bedroom hasn't been rebuilt since. My granny never let anyone touch that.'

'Did she know . . . as a child?'

Joanie lowered her head and hunched her knees forward. Without her replying I could see the small community on that bridge ninety years before. A child in a white dress surrounded by whispers, staring across the river valley at the trees blowing above the locked gates. I found I stopped myself from imagining Joanie's great grandmother. Perhaps I didn't want to face the intensity of her yearning for her child among those trapped inmates, or maybe I was frightened of putting madness on Joanie's features.

'You're not lying to me, are you?'

I knew the question hurt her and was sorry I had spoken. For once it didn't need an answer. I no longer thought of manipulation. I felt something had been stripped away, I was finally coming closer to whoever Joanie really was.

'It's easy for you,' she said, 'with no ties to nobody. I've never heard you mention a mother or a father or any goddamn thing. You think you are free, don't you, above all this but tell me, do you ever feel anything?'

Her words hurt the more for echoing what had been in my head, and we were even now. You are born alone and you die that way. The boy alone in the church where the winter light faded had given way to the youth running through fields not towards a rendezvous with his gods but away from them. The question I had promised myself that every morning I would answer, to believe in something or to believe in nothing, the question I had put off for all my life, the only question that had finally mattered. The funny thing was that up there it felt like I had stopped running. The thirteen-year-old boy wakes at thirty-one on a dirty, littered headland. *Do you ever really feel anything?* I did for a moment there. A sudden closeness with something I could not explain.

Joanie stumbled on through crooked briars and dumped litter to the far edge of the headland which ended with the stumps of severed trees. I still didn't know why she had brought me this way. She slid down and almost fell into the stream running through the small untouched meadow where two horses slept upright. When I climbed after her she kissed me for a moment and then, uncharacteristically, took my hand. Neither horse moved as we passed close to them. It felt eerie to walk through high grass in the midst of a city with the distant lights of factories and houses and streets encircling us.

The back wall to her cottage was low, the garden slightly overgrown. I was sobering up but still followed her through the window of the old back room, undressing in the darkness without making a sound. There was something illicit there which made our sex seem special. I could have been a gentleman caller stealthily stealing her virtue. It was a fantasy which I felt we were both sharing, but I wasn't sure if she was controlling it by her muted sighs, her half glances of fear or vulnerability towards the door. It was different from any other time, before or since, with her or with anyone. It was as serious as death and just as inconceivable. I kept my eyes closed. I felt no longer just myself, but like a man from another time, a man with a name or secret I should know which erased itself from my mind as I spent.

I must have slept again for no more than an hour. The room was still dark when I half woke up, the pain in my head intense. Bridget was crouched in the corner. She looked up bewildered; it was obvious she had not slept. I felt overwhelmed with contempt for myself, with sudden pity for her.

'I'm going mad, tutor,' she said. 'Is there to be no help for me? It was just a game I played when I used to be left alone. In the years after Mama died, just me and Dada here, me trying to be a woman, look after him. Did you not invent things when you were a child, people, friends who never really existed?'

Although I tried to speak, all that came was a dry choking sound in my throat. I glanced towards the floor, both relieved to make out the shape of my clothes there and ashamed that my first thought was my own safety, though I could not have arisen if I wished to.

'It was just a game I used to play out walking. Playing up among the stones where the old house used to be. They used to tell me not to go there, that I'd remember bad things, but I remember nothing from that time. Used to pretend I'd meet her there, always waiting for me in the stones. Her funny way of talking like nursery rhymes, only black and dark and terrible. It was like she needed things, words, people's names, names of fields, townlands. Like she knew of nothing herself, only words I didn't understand, makey-up ones. It was just a game, tutor, like playing with an imaginary doll. Then one day she followed me home.'

'Please, Bridget, listen to me,' I mumbled, trying to rise up on one elbow and failing. 'I give you my word. There is nothing in this room to be scared of.'

I am unsure if my voice even carried. Bridget bit at her knuckles, then raised her hand and banged it against the wall.

'Babyface I used to call her. Tap at the window, Babyface, tap lightly when Dada's asleep and I will let you in. *I'll dare you, I'll dare you to do bold things.* Like I had to tell her how everything felt. I'd sit here at night inventing words for her to say, laughing at them. Tutor, I didn't know the words that I made up. I said one to my father once and he slapped me across the mouth, "Where did you hear that, you filthy little girl?" How could I know a word that I have never heard? You've read the books, tutor, you tell me that.'

I felt as if I were being lulled by opium into a pit that her words were echoing down. And the more I tried to speak and reassure her, the further I sank. I wanted to listen, I wanted to help her, yet sleep was my only master and I could only struggle to delay its call.

'It began with funny words but soon she took over my thoughts. Thoughts I could never have dreamt, of men's bodies, always whispering about them, *Johnny, Johnny* over and over. Her voice was in my skull and it never let go. Even in Mass it was mocking me, almost making me choke on the Sacred Host. Like she never heard of God, there was no heaven, no hell, just an emptiness, an ache like some black gaping hole. I wake at night-time and I can see her here, a shadow on the wall, a dark silhouette, crouched up, rocking back and forth. It frightens me so much, makes me feel . . . like I were a ghost and she the live one. Oh, God help me, Sir, she's here with us now. Can you not see anything, tutor, do you not even have the slightest fear?'

But my eyes would not stay open. I tried to turn my head, glimpsed the bare ceiling and part of the wall and after that I sank into sleep again.

Afterwards I lay swamped in the sensation of heat and drying sweat, and longed for a cigarette. The feeling that I should know something still lingered. I was sobering up fast.

'Is this room haunted?' I whispered for no reason and Joanie shook her head.

'There are no ghosts,' she said. 'That's just rubbish they invented to make videos.'

'How do you know?'

'Of course I know. If there were they could queue up in this room. Now let's not talk about it.'

She sulked for a few moments before she spoke again.

'Every Sunday my mother was locked in here for four or five hours at a time when my granny and granda went out. She told me once. They'd dress up and take a tram to town, have tea and cakes in a hotel. My granny did it. Granda was just a weak giant of a man who worked himself to death. My granny still gets his pension. She gets some of my father's too, paid over to her. All those different pensions from dead men.'

I remembered a film I'd seen about an old woman who killed her lodgers and kept them preserved under the floorboards. The eyes of the young man who was next in line came back to me as he pulled the boards up and stared down.

'Are you sure she can't hear us?'

'She's deaf, stone deaf as the wall.'

A night bird spoke on a branch in the garden. I could hear nothing of the traffic which must be passing on the carriageway. There were no lights visible from the window. When the bird stopped I could hear the noise of the stream down in the gully and nothing else except Joanie's breath.

'Haunted isn't the right word,' she said suddenly. 'I don't know the word but that isn't it. When I was young I used to pretend that there were two girls trapped in here. A weaker girl who was old-fashioned and good, a real little Victorian Miss, and the other could make her do things she didn't want. The other would punish her for no reason whenever I was sad, would take out all my fears and pains on her for me, make her live them for me, make her do things I wanted to know and feel but was too young to. The other was like . . . she was like nothing, like a face with no features, laughing and cackling, tormenting the girl. You know how a child is cruel, mindlessly tearing the legs off daddy-long-legs to see what it would do. That was me. It seemed almost real at the time when I was half asleep but it was just a game in my head. I'd forgotten all about it until the day Johnny Whelan found the room where that girl was locked up on the hill.'

'Why?' I said. 'What's that got to do with it?'

'I don't know,' Joanie whispered. 'Just felt this awful sense that . . .'

Joanie crossed her hands on the pillow and cradled her head. She stared at the ceiling although nothing was there. I waited for her to finish the sentence but instead, after a few moments, she began to speak about her mother's death in a low voice, about how when the labour pains started her granny had ordered her father to stay at home, but her mother refused to leave without him. They shouted in the kitchen while the pains came quicker and the taxi meter ticked away like a time bomb on the hill outside. Finally they all travelled in the taxi together. Her father in front, Joanie squeezed between the two women. Her mother was sweating, her dress damp when Joanie leaned her head against it.

'Soft I remember, like nothing else was ever soft. And wet like your body would be after a shower.'

I shifted sideways and stretched my knee towards her. Joanie wrapped her thighs about it and I felt the weight of her breasts against my chest. Her body was hot like a child with fever, her voice the faintest whisper coming through a tangle of damp hair.

'When we reached the hospital the shouting really started. The doctor, a little Asian, said that only husbands could be present at the birth. My granny was furious. Mammy was put on a stretcher. She kissed me and took Daddy's hand. I spent an hour in the husbands' waiting-room with all that thick smoke till my granny gave up arguing and took me home.'

A haemorrhage from a ruptured womb the doctors called it, a rare event now, the whole hospital shocked by it. The baby survived in intensive care, the mother died after two days in a coma. Her grandmother blamed it on her father for being in the labour ward where a man had no business. She badgered him back to work the day after the funeral and then took all his wife's possessions, burning the clothes in the garden, hiding the presents he had given her. His own belongings were heaped in the room that we were lying in and Joanie's bed moved into the room where her parents had slept. The bright cot he had bought for Joanie was smashed for firewood, her granny's old heavy one taken down from the attic and put beside the old woman's bed.

'I never knew the woman could have such strength,' Joanie whispered. 'She was over eighty, yet she was hauling things like a young man.'

She had ripped off the kingsize sheet that held the two single beds together. Joanie claimed she shredded it between her bony fingers. Joanie sat on his bed, clutching her favourite doll until her father walked up from the bus stop and stared at the mess of shirts and socks on the floor.

'He had that look you see in horror videos,' she said. 'When the aliens have sucked the blood from a man and he's walking around all rubbery with dry air in his veins and when his eyes hit the sunlight you know they'll crumble.'

Joanie's eyes were dry and hard as if they would never blink again.

'She gave him his meals in silence and then left him to rot in this room, badgering him if he went into the kitchen or other rooms, complaining if he went out of the house. After he died she wanted to close off the room but I fought to get it back. I can still smell his sick breath here as he wasted away to death.'

'How did he die?' I thought of that momentary sense I had had of being someone else. Was it something of him I had felt?

'Six years he came in and out when I was barely allowed a glance at him. Then one day he collapsed in work. The doctors can call it what they want but I know the name for it. Not that he got the doctors or nurses or medicine in this place. My granny wouldn't allow it and he never went against her. He knew this wasn't his house, his home. Only once did he defy her – that day the papers were full of photographs of the girl's room that Johnny found he sent me out for them all. He had some coins hidden under the mattress. I remember the pages spread out on the bed before him. My granny was in like a hen, clucking at the cost of them, but he ignored her, just looking from one photograph to the next and when his eyes looked up at me they were weak and yellow.'

I saw him, as she spoke, in this very bed a few years before, saw the thousand and a half nights he must have passed alone, the arc of light under the door, the sounds of his own children's voices coming through the wood. Not even a photograph of him remained, Joanie said, but I could picture him, a thin man with a mousy moustache, a model worker, popular and overlooked. What were the small triumphs he set against the humiliation of every day? The chance a child might smile at him when her granny's back was turned, a few moments sneaked at a doorway watching his daughters lost in sleep.

'I knew he was dying that day,' Joanie said, 'and when I looked at my granny I knew she knew as well. I told her he was sick as we left the room. "Sick of going to work and earning his money like a Christian," she said. "He's not sick of being a nuisance here." She was letting him die, punishing him for something. Knowing he hadn't the courage or strength to phone a doctor for himself.'

Joanie was silent. I knew why he had kept those newspapers about the woman's daughter. They were his identity too, the story of his entombment. Joanie said the room had not been touched since his death and in whatever moonlight remained it could have been an anonymous hotel bedroom with just a bed and chest of drawers. He must have known his fate, what reason would he have to pretend or hope he might recover? All he had were those newspapers under the bed, within reach at night when despair got too much, the knowledge that someone else had lain in such a room so close to him and that her name at least had one day been spoken. Did he welcome death, wait for it like a friend, or fear it? Suddenly I wanted that feeling to have been him, that room to be haunted. I wanted his ghost to appear, to be able to look at his eyes, to say something; not that I understand or feel what you felt, just that I know you once existed.

I woke shortly before dawn to find the window open. I knew she was gone before looking around. I dressed quickly and went in search of her. I no longer cared who saw me now. I just wanted to find her, make sure she was safe. I knew she would be sitting up on the headland above the stream which flickered through the trees below. She had a blanket wrapped around her shoulders and was staring across at the blackened rocks on the far slope beyond her father's cottage. I called and she looked up with a wide vacant smile. Her face looked radiant and childlike, yet something in that glazed happiness frightened me more than the haunted look she had previously worn.

'You'll catch cold,' I said, 'you must come down.'

'But I don't feel cold,' she replied, 'I feel so warm.'

There were goose pimples along her arms. I heard a sudden noise behind me; young Turlough had scrambled up through the wood. He stopped, startled to see us, and looked scared as he darted away through the trees. I got Bridget to her feet.

'Come on down, Bridget, your father will be coming home soon.'

'Poor Dada, left all alone.'

She walked with her head high in slow exaggerated movements as though stepping through water. We crossed the meadow, this time together with neither of us speaking. She was humming to herself, gazing around with that terrible heightened elation. A crowd had gathered at the back of the cottages. I thought they were watching us but then saw how their eyes were fixed on the hollow beneath the bridge. A battered cart had been backed down to the stream's edge. The driver jerked the horse forward by the harness and it clambered up on to the road, breathing heavily through its nostrils at the effort. Old potato sacks were heaped over something in the cart. The small crowd blessed themselves as the wheels creaked past.

Bridget's father turned from the cart and, seeing us, ran forward to take her in his arms. His face was white from dust and worry as neighbours crowded round with soothing clucking noises. I waited for the blows to come. He drew his daughter under one arm and turned towards me.

'Thank you for bringing her back, Sir,' he said. 'Where did you find her? With old Matthew found drowned I've been nearly out of my mind with worry.'

Bridget looked up serenely.

'I got lost on the hill, Dada, and the gentleman showed

me home. Up in the woods. I shouldn't have gone wandering.'

Her father patted her and turned towards the house with the neighbouring women following. An old fellow paused and spat companionably at the grass.

'Was it up yonder above the dairy you found her?'

I nodded nervously.

'Aye, that's where I find her myself often enough. There or over by the old house. Half simple she is but a good little girl all the same. Takes notions about herself but you know, when she was born she was the most ordinary of children.'

'The mother's death, maybe? Here in the cottage.'

He looked surprised that I knew of it. He pointed up beyond the cottages towards the crest of the hill overlooking the new cemetery. I could see the outline of an overgrown path leading to the pile of black stones Bridget had been staring at.

'That happened up there, well over a decade ago now. I don't think her father was right in the head for a long while after, the poor man. An oul' tinker who passed filled his head with nonsense. Do you know what them people do when a person dies, eh? Only pile everything the person owned up in their wicker tent and set the tent and all in it alight. Well, I suppose there's no fights about who gets what with everything burnt to ash, but it's no wonder they're always squatting on the roadside without a farthing in the arse of their pants. That might be all right for the likes of them, but it was sheer madness for settled folk.'

As he spoke the pile of black rocks became the outline of burnt walls.

'If a man isn't used to whiskey he shouldn't take it,' he said and spat again. 'If you ask me it was the second fire drove the child wild. Every scrap of her mother's clothes piled up in the kitchen and paraffin oil splashed over them. Off she took by herself screaming so it took half the village combing the hillside to find her. Up there she was on that headland by the dairy gibbering away in the cold of dawn. The old women around here say a changeling came and stole her body, if you believe that talk. They wanted to tie her down and burn the spirit out of her with a hot poker. All of them cackling away like hens in the doorway. Her father had to beat them away. He called a real doctor and paid him with silver. He used words we didn't understand but can't you see from the cut of the child? It's pure madness, man, and it will not be long taking over. It's the gates of the madhouse for her and her father's old age to be spent alone. Good day to you now.'

He turned abruptly and walked towards the cottages. The damp dew was penetrating through my boots. I was the villain and yet had escaped retribution. I stood excluded from the villagers by my accent and clothes. But more than everything I had seen or done it was Bridget's words that haunted me. Standing in the brightness of that morning, I could sense the emptiness, the black hole she spoke of, as though it would engulf her and myself and our entire world. I climbed up on to the road and tried to walk briskly away. I stopped at the bridge and looked down at the mud. I could see the marks of the wheels where they had pulled the old man's body out and there, like the only evidence that the night had taken place, were the crumpled white cigarettes I had left in the woods for him. I checked my pocket suddenly and felt a stab of fear when I realized the cigarette case was missing.

We were both silent in the bed, thinking of her father. My penis had hardened again in that moist embrace, only now it felt like incest as she rolled me over and climbed on top. I wanted to say something, explain how I felt. She stretched herself so tight it seemed my foreskin would burst.

'You're different from the rest,' she said. 'I'd have a child for you if you wanted.'

'You have a child already, or have you forgotten?'

'I'd have another one for you, another daughter.'

'And how do you know I'd marry you?'

'I never asked you to. I'll be your mistress, your best one, even bring you other girls if you wanted.'

Her breath was coming faster and suddenly she started to moan. I tried to hush her but she grabbed my fists and pushed them back against the pillow. The sheet had ridden off her, her skin glistened like a drenched leaf in a deodorant commercial. I felt her eyes no longer saw me, her voice as she rocked herself was like an old mourner keening. There was a light on the landing and the door slid open. Joanie never even turned to look at her granny as she pushed herself towards her climax. The old woman was shrunken and wrinkled like a grape left too long in the sun. I might have been invisible as she stared at her granddaughter's buttocks. Joanie came with a low animal cry. I was still stiff but numb as if my penis was no longer mine. When I came it was like something frozen had slid out from me.

'You bitch,' the old woman said. 'In this, your father's room.'

Joanie ceased moving and straightened her back up. She looked over her shoulder tauntingly.

'Don't you mention his name in here. At least I know who my own father was.'

I had never felt as strange as this, like I were dead and could still hear voices around my bedside. The awful feeling returned that this had already happened if I could only remember, that it wasn't Joanie's father but something else, a memory, a dream I had forgotten which haunted me. There was a slurping noise as Joanie slid off me and my penis slipped out of her. The two women stared at each other. I could see Joanie's features on the old woman like a crinkled photocopy. The old woman looked down at Joanie's clothes scattered along with the contents of her bag on the floor.

'That's my mother's cigarette case,' she muttered weakly, 'I told you before you can't have it.'

Joanie's teeth flashed above me as she smiled. She knelt up now so that no part of her body even touched mine.

'I said at least I know who my own father was.'

The old woman looked down again at her worn slippers. She shuffled awkwardly, then turned and was gone. Joanie fell back on the mattress beside me. I heard her giggle to herself. I knew I was redundant. She was buried among the bedclothes, the odd sliver of flesh glimpsed in the moonlight like a corpse in a shallow grave after weeks of torrential rain. I could hear her laugh as I put my clothes on and walked out through the hall. I stopped at the front door. Joanie's little sister was in the hall in her pyjamas staring at me. I strained to hear any sound of a baby. I heard nothing and realized how little I was sure of.

At the waste ground near the traffic lights a bulldozer had eaten away the last of the famine mound Joanie had told me about. A new billboard was advertising more town houses. In the ploughed earth there were plastic markers and a row of white crosses. I knew that they only marked out foundations but I wanted to tell myself that one was for her father and the others for all the women and men whose lives had been buried alive in rooms where the sun rarely shone.

The Whelan boy was standing on the corner, his face bloated from whatever drugs the clinic fed him on. He was staring at the broken pillars of the entrance to what had once been the asylum. I didn't know if he thought anything but perhaps he knew that that was where he would have wound up a hundred years before. When I passed he turned to glance at me as though I were familiar. My cock hurt, I wanted a cigarette badly, I wanted to wash out my mouth. I had passed him and was looking for a taxi back to town when I stopped.

I thought of all the evil I knew of in the world, not the great wars and famines, but the thousands of lives crippled in the name of family love, of that violence never spoken, rarely made physical, the slights and silences twisting like a knife into a loved one's flesh. I thought of those back there; Joanie naked on her back in one room, her granny lying like a corpse in another, with a faded pattern of roses on a wall between them, her sister still standing in the hall, a doll clutched to her breast the way Joanie had cuddled one as she waited for her father to come home from work two days after her mother's death. And though I was about to be driven away under the cold yellow lights, I knew that I had not escaped, I would never shake the feeling of having been an accessory to a crime.

Like a small sharp pearl she came back to me, as cold as her age. And yet it wasn't her that was holding me there. I waited at the corner and felt again that sensation I had not been able to explain. For a moment it seemed as if it were the presence I had dreamt of as a child on those damp roads, not a god now, but something lost and overlooked, whose feet inaudibly beat with my feet on the hard pavement, whose breath panted in the moonlight with mine. I turned to look back. Only the Whelan kid was there with his idiotic stare.

So why did I feel I had finally kept that rendezvous? For one brief second I allowed myself to imagine I was not just a fluke of biology and chance. Like Joanie's father, consoled by the thought of other lives, I felt suddenly one of a long line that stretched behind me and before me, I as much a speck in their minds as they were in mine, that if I could only grasp them this would all make sense to me. Then I shook the feeling. I wished I could believe in ghosts, that I did have some connection with that place, but I knew it was just drink and physical signals from my body that this madness would have to stop.

The nightclub would still be thumping out music when I got home, like a dentist's drill trying to root out an aching pain. Couples would clutter up the quays, searching for taxis, trying to cling on to the ambience there. I knew I would never see Joanie again. Her name would appear on the attendance book till all her sick allowance ran out. Some nights I would wake in a strange sweat. Phrases would come back to me, parts of her body, the way her eyes looked. *You're the most beautiful man I've ever known. I'd have a child for you, a daughter.* How much was real or at least meant at that moment and how much was I simply an instrument of revenge?

A taxi came down the carriageway and I hailed it, music blaring on the car stereo, the driver grinning at my dishevelled hair. He tore up the hill towards the all-night garage, his fingers tapping on the wheel, and when I looked through the rear-view mirror the Whelan kid still stood, like Joanie had once done, shrinking into a motionless speck that never budged until I was gone.

The early weeks after that night felt unreal, waiting for a knock at the room, the constabulary or my employer. Then the cycles of ordinary life drew me back in. The closeness of my escape startled me back to my senses. Bridget's illness passed through the house in a whisper, a new girl started, I heard the sound of young voices laughing from downstairs. If I did not forget her, then in time I learned to live with the memory; I felt a grief when I thought of her and quiet relief that I was not implicated; I woke occasionally unable to prevent myself lingering on some detail of our night together. I managed to avoid that road, the row of cottages, the arched bridge, the asylum walls.

Fashions change and the rich feign new interests and passions. I still remember the shock when I heard the faltering phrase of Gaelic spoken by a visitor in the drawing-room. It is quite the rage now in literary circles. Five guineas I received for my first work of translation, the tales from the west of Ireland which my mother spluttered out to us in that tenement, now set down in stiff, antiquated English. They are praised in a small way as long as I curtail them, take out the native sweat and dirt and put in noble peasants with flighty words. I was born at the tail-end of a famine nobody wants to be reminded of.

Instead I give them heroic vassals as pure and forced as Bridget's last smile.

I have long left Shallon House, and now teach only Latin, like a rich version of Hegerty, in several of the neighbouring big houses. Although I still work mainly for Protestants, I have learned to keep close to the priests again. A Catholic with such a grasp of Gaelic and Latin is rare. We're growing rich as a religion, anxious for coats of arms as good as any Englishman's. The fact that I work for Protestants makes me a prize to be displayed. I tour the new houses, giving them inscriptions of their clans in Latin and Gaelic, occasionally bearing Homer to their children.

Eighteen months after Bridget entered the asylum I married Mary, a good and simple woman, and bought this cottage off Washerwoman's Hill, blessed by the convent gates and secured by the barracks. The tram terminates on the hill. Beyond that, although I never ventured there, the hill slopes down towards the cottages by the bridge.

The labouring men in the fields salute me now. Barre, the grocer, tries to recruit me for his campaign against the extravagance of asphalting the paths. He tells me the gossip of the lower orders who pass up and down the hillside. One spring evening, three years after I moved there, as he brought me to the door to show his esteem for my custom, Bridget's father passed, exhausted looking, curled up on the back of a cartload of flour.

'Away down Slut's Alley that man there goes,' Barre laughed. 'The drivers still give him lifts in the carts though he's long sacked, but I don't approve at all. I tell you, Slut's Alley could have been named after his clan down by the bridge. He has a daughter across the road from him, locked up in the madhouse. Did you know that now?'

I gazed after the cart, neither shaking nor nodding my head.

'And a wee slip of a granddaughter tucked away at home in a room.'

It was like the man had punched me. I tried not to stagger, reaching back to grasp the door behind me.

'A granddaughter you say?'

'Surely you've heard tell of it? Sure, it's a disgrace on the whole neighbourhood. They're clearing away the mud heaps and yet letting people away with the likes of that. The man's stubborn and dumb. My God, there were nuns down to him and priests, but sure even if the Archbishop of Dublin had descended on his cottage nothing was good enough for the man but to rear the child himself. He lost his job and all, only now gets the odd bit of work as a night-watchman. He locks her up when he goes to work. The neighbours hear her crying all alone in the back room by herself.'

'But you said his daughter's in the asylum?'

'She delivered in the asylum, seven and a half months after she was brought in.'

'Who is the father?'

I wanted him to answer me, I needed a name. Barre laughed and slapped me on the shoulder.

'When the harlot was around, Slut's Alley must have fairly earned its name.'

He moved inside chuckling to serve a customer. I took my *Evening Mail* and began my walk up the hill towards my wife with our child growing inside her. The long months of disappointment, the uncertainty and then exhilaration at the news, the nights in our bed discussing names, planning a bright white future. But was I a father already, a daughter, born of seed I had thought spilt over her mother's belly and breasts, growing in poverty that my own child would escape from? Or was Barre right, was I just one of many lured to that room, spun stories of shapes on walls? She had cried out, claimed to be a virgin, but could I remember whether there was blood? That night she had run through the meadow was there somebody in her room, her father perhaps, a bullying neighbour who knew she was alone? Had she been forced to commit an act against her will and turned to me with wild stories, hoping somehow I would save her?

I went over every possibility, yet that cold dread never left my stomach. Everything I had worked for, the secure walls and careful future, seemed taken from me and yet I could not even be sure of what I was guilty. And now another thought plagued me like a wasp brushing about in my skull. Was she committed because she was deranged or because they had discovered the child growing inside her?

I have tried to shake off these thoughts, but now at night I am haunted by what haunted her, by unseen figures, by thoughts that make sense to no one. And I realize it is not the ghosts locked in the past that should frighten us, but those of the unborn, the undreamt of, the future ones beyond our control or comprehension who will remember or forget, forgive or condemn us.

Each morning my wife fusses over the simple daily things, my new pupils wait, growing older and more sullen. And all my Latin verbs cannot save me from these thoughts. They flood in when I pause between tenses. I stand on the waxed floor among wooden desks, the air bright, shafts of sunlight sliding across the wall. And I can hear my voice as though it belonged to someone else, someone I was once, reciting Latin. But I can feel a darkness enveloping me, can feel her limbs sweating, the tightness of her cunt as though it were drawing my world in and casting me out into a space without walls or sense.

I want to run from it and yet I want that abandonment back just once before my youth flickers out into monotony. I want to cast this world to hell but am frightened to lose my lowly perch above the footmen in the houses I teach in. When my pupils are gone I sit on in those rooms, trace the carved initials on the wood with my finger. A.J.C. 2/6/95, S.H.C. 21/12/96. How self-important their initials look, carved with contempt, the certain knowledge of their worth. It should console me that they will be swept into the furnace that I sense is coming, and yet they are what define me and when they are gone all trace of me will be erased as well.

I want to be remembered and yet I don't know by

whom. Which daughter, if I have two, will find me the least unfathomable? If they too have children will they in turn honestly believe that I existed? I don't mean times of birth and death, but the thousands of insignificant acts that made up my life. If these words survive they may grasp certain set pieces, a figure by the window where young faces bend reluctantly over their books, an ostracized man in a corner of a tavern, even the morning I leaned forth to call down to the bewildered girl. But will they really conceive of the seconds that can never be described, the constant heartbeat, the blood pumping, my breath even as I write this turning to vapour in the chill of my room? I am trying to see you, grandson or great grandson or great granddaughter, am trying to speak to you, to imagine your world. Yesterday I realized I did not know my mother's father's name, had never asked her, had never even thought of that man. But when you become a father death ceases to be just a word.

I have tried to break the habit, but most evenings at a certain time I can no longer bear to sit in this cottage. I look at my daughter in her wooden cot, her hands thrown back behind her head, lips pursed as she sleeps. I pause at the loft door a moment, hoping her serenity can quench my unease, then I turn and whistle for the dog.

It has been the longest autumn I've ever known, the leaves massed knee-high at the base of the trunks. Night has descended with a mist which hints of rain to come. The dog whines for home but still I wait beneath the half-bare branches. Before me is the asylum where Bridget sleeps or lies awake beneath the high arched window of a cell. Behind me the waters froth over the rocks beneath the bridge. Footsteps pass, solitary and youthful from the sound of them. I step back and do not turn until the figure of the young man is indecipherable, a farm labourer heading home or a vagabond perhaps, passing the cottage where a child is locked up whose eyes may perhaps mirror my own. The young man stops. There is something familiar about him. If it were not so dark I would swear he was watching. He turns to vanish over the brow of the hill. Are mother and daughter awake at this moment, I wonder, both facing each other, staring up through windows they cannot open, neither aware that I am under this tree, caught for ever between them, powerless to know or to change anything? I whistle for the dog and, as we walk home, I am filled with an unease that we are somehow both ghosts, that we will never arrive back to the warmth of that kitchen where Mary waits even after we think we have reached there, that we are trapped for eternity on this corner, indistinct and lost beneath the first squalls of evening rain.

PART THREE

The Crystal Rivulet

I can still sense it here, Johnny, feel it in my blood as it flows beneath this roadway. Thirty years since last June the stream has been buried – I remember coming up from my cottage that morning to watch the workmen smoothing over the tarmacadam with the children from the new houses gathered in a crowd – but I can sense it now swirling down the bank through the underground pipe, past the roots of the fir trees in your granny's garden and slopping underneath the very foundations of the room you sleep in.

It's my secret, this twisting water path hidden under all these houses and roads, there are few left alive who could follow it still. But every night I walk its length, naming the runs and trout pools that have vanished, recording the name of each for nobody. And one day soon you will know it too, you'll feel its pull beneath your feet like a diviner, stumble through every night-lit street again and again waiting for the moment of certainty when you will know you are standing above the exact spot, until you can trace its route at night in the darkness of your mind.

I could walk for miles each night once. It's all a single man can do when his mind lays siege to him. The vital thing now is not to fall – death I can tolerate, it is to be crippled which terrifies me. The joints stiffen in this autumn weather, I have to rest to catch my breath after every twenty strides, but I can see my destination now after all these empty years. I've not much longer to walk, a few more miles and my task is done. Every day for these past few months I've thought, *why you of all of them?* And every night I've stood here in the shadows of your house, like a young man courting a shy bride, desperate for a glimpse of an arm, a bare shoulder, anything before your light is switched off.

I'm pressed against the wall of this laneway where the shadows hide me from the road. I know how dangerous it is, the eve of Hallowe'en, every scrap of waste ground and every derelict house looted for timber. I can hear the gangs passing, the clank of bottles and their heavy laughter, but it's all that's left to me now, your framed square of curtained light floating like some night sailor in the blackness of the wall. I long for these moments, even more than your chance visits in the afternoon, they keep me warm as though just by gazing up towards your room I am sharing an intimacy with you. I spend the days not daring to count the time until I can begin this walk and when your light goes out I am dead and trapped already in the deaf suffocation of the earth.

Only the headlights of the huge trucks can catch me here, their rickety beams bumping and shifting over the road's uneven surface. They stumble on to me for just an instant, ancient battered hat, long black overcoat and hawthorn stick, with my dark face screwed up to stare back at them sweeping on towards the traffic lights. From Meath and Monaghan they come, sealed containers of machinery and heaped carcasses still saturated with blood, as they head towards the docks. I can see them coming in my mind, swaying across the night over the flat road I often travelled to be hired out as a boy, through Slane and Ashbourne, the white mist gathering in the fields like a foretaste of dawn as they trundle onwards towards the first street lights on the edge of the city, the sudden wavecrest of houses and my old face perpetually caught against the wall.

Some drivers raise their hands from the wheel, they've become like friends now, messengers from outside, their wheels trembling as they wait for the lights to change. I shuffle forward awkwardly on my stick as though trying to communicate with them: wait for me, I too want to change, to pass on, to die, to break from the purgatory of this place. The green light floods on, they surge forward and I am left behind.

Ever since the morning when his grandmother led him up the overgrown path and into the oppressive stillness of the house where the woman and her daughter lived, the same nightmare had become his constant nocturnal companion. It haunted Johnny Whelan so much that he would lie awake for hours after he went to bed with the light on in his room and his heart pounding as he tried to still the buzzing in his head and focus his thoughts on what was happening to him. He had to fight it, stay calm, tell nobody. The red tablets were piled up in their jar by the bed like the moons of Mars that had crashed from their orbit. Eventually he would swallow the last one and force himself to switch off the light and allow sleep to take possession of him.

Then the dream would return in which he was still awake and lying in an unnaturally pitched blackness which obliterated all the familiar landmarks of the room. Was he at home in his parents' house, the childhood bedroom that was his no longer? He shook off the sensation, he knew where he was, the room he had slept in every night since his father's death, the room in which his own mother had lain awake after dates as a single girl. Gradually from his left a tiny column of light began to glimmer through the curtains and he was able to distinguish the shape of the room again. He stared in fascination at the faint reflection of light, like phosphorescence, like a luminous statue from Lourdes, which shone from the far side of the glass. The curtains seemed about to separate by themselves and yet never moved, like Christ's eyes in a religious painting if you stared closely at them. The light terrified him and yet he was drawn towards it. There was no sound in the house, as though his room had become detached from the lives around him. If he shouted he knew nobody would hear and when he tried he found that his throat was so dry no sound would come from it.

There was just him and the light shining dull and patient through the glass, ebbing and quivering like a flame. He wanted to stay away from it but his mind seemed to have lost control over his limbs. His bare feet slid from the sheets on to the cool lino and he stood gazing at the illuminated pattern on the curtain. He felt his hair stiffen and his legs tremble as he moved towards the window. Somehow it seemed as if his future waited there, embedded in that flame weaving in the shape of a figure through the cloth, that the explanation of these last few months burned within that light, but if he chose to pull the curtain aside he could never return to the safety of the world he had known.

What does it want of me? he repeated in his mind, *what does it want*? He gazed in horror at his right hand which crept towards the curtain and just when his fingers began to close over the knotted cord he was caught, lifted up and flung weightlessly into the air. He hung swaying between the floor and ceiling in an enveloping flush of heat from the light which ignited to fill the entire window and then retreated away from the house. And always at this stage he remembered that it was a dream, the same dream, and he would be both relieved and furious with himself for being fooled by it again. He would wake with that strange warmth draining from his limbs to lie in the dark bedroom, knowing that he was too old at sixteen to cry out or to be scared, afraid to give them any ammunition for their injections and red tablets.

And as he lay there struggling to be calm, he would always remember the slow walk with his grandmother up the path to the woman's house, sparkling with slivers of glass, and into the dank hallway, the cluster of hushed women unsure of what to do next, and how, when they opened the living-room door to stare at the smears of blood and smashed ornaments, he had walked by himself up the stairs, feeling the wood creak beneath him, and turned his head at the top as though drawn by compulsion to look in through the open bedroom door. How long had he sat on the top step, not needing to go any further, waiting for his grandmother to discover him, for the women to come and stare through the open bedroom door where the single shaft of light lit the fading colours of the lino? The moment was frozen in his mind as if his life before that had just been a preparation for the instant when, gazing down at the dusty yellow sunlight entering the hallway, he had imagined from behind him a sudden sharp pain like a child's bony fingers pinching his back. And then slowly he had turned his head.

I was named after a lake that wells up during the winter rains to disappear in springtime again. *Turlough*, my father said, the only word of Gaelic he knew. This was his favourite street, leading down through hawthorn bushes across the small bridge to the Jolly Toper.

They've torn it apart now, the carriageway has sliced open its soul. This clanging metal bridge links the two halves, the noise of my boots and stick telegraphed through the steel to echo down at the far end. The top of the trucks almost touch my feet, the bridge trembling in their slipstream. The view from up here is like I remember as a child before the estates cut off the sweep of hills down to the city. Ten minutes it often takes me to crawl across its back. I feel like I'm crossing the hunched skeleton of some metallic dinosaur, the ghost of a future age who came this far and withered in the dead world of what was once my home.

Those cottages down below, where I often sat watching the carts creak in from the countryside. The Ferret Casey tuning his fiddle while his wife fetched the oil lamp down. The roofs are gone from them now, a single rafter standing like a naked bone. The children have torn the corrugated iron from the windows to climb inside. You can see the glint of smashed bottles there, the blackened stains in a corner where somebody lit a fire and still a small square of wallpaper hanging on one wall like an epithet. Any last timbers have been torn away since yesterday, are loaded now on unlit bonfires beneath the night sky. I've watched them sink this far, pitying their dilapidation, but now they will survive to see me buried.

Past the pub with the overgrown lane and around by the trees. I'll halt by the old Protestant church to get my breath back. That rasping hurts my throat, each night it grows harder to walk but I'll finish my rounds again, I'll keep faith with the past. The church is rarely used now with so few Protestants left, not like when the Archbishop and Lord Chancellor had their big houses here. They've placed wire mesh over the stained glass. It must break up the moonlight straining down the aisle inside, stretching from the gold dais wrought into the shape of an eagle in flight, past the empty pews to the cupped stone of the baptism font.

Often when I listen out here I catch the splash of water there, no cry, no name, just the pouring of water over a skull which is gone. The moonlight never touches the side walls, the elaborate stone carvings carried from the ruined church to those fallen asleep or taken into the Lord's care, their titles and virtues etched into the white stone. And beside the altar, the most simple plaque: *Elizabeth Morris, National Teacher in this parish, 1890–1933*. I remember her hunched figure at the top of the classroom, staring through spectacles at the children of the children she once taught. And a bright sweet proffered to the barefoot Catholic boy that was me, standing there, after running from Shallon House with a note for the child of one of the big farmers nearby.

I've never known whose feet they are, but each night I hear them, the right leg dragging a little as the footsteps pace down the aisle, one of the hundreds of journeys never completed through the village. That exhausted horse straining up the hill on the Main Street, her caked mane and face flecked with muck and sweat as she presses towards the trough she will never reach on the fair-green outside the pub; the fair-haired child with consumption coughing for eternity in the top bedroom of the house on the corner; the dwarf almost hidden by the parapet of the stone bridge that has vanished; the contorted face of the lunatic racing through the garden of Farnham where foreign nuns now walk in the convent; the foot soldier, speared by a sharpened stick when the siege was broken, still twisting towards death on the shoulder of the new carriageway; the youth's hand on fire when they melted the lead from the roof of the great house to make bullets; the terrified woman peering from the deep-set window of a vanished cottage in the floodlit supermarket car-park, keeping a vigil for her husband's return. These ones I feel I can see, but there are other more indistinct, ancient shapes without even the memory of features now.

The list is so long I find it hard to remember each one. All the way from the dying square of light in Johnny's window to the bedroom of the cabin where I was born, I try to think of each of them, like an old woman in church with her litany of saints' names. I shamble down these alien streets, named after patriots and flowering trees. My legs ache with the strain but I remember them still. This was my home once; I knew the eye in the knot of every tree, the moss sheltering in the stones of each laneway. It's yours now, Johnny, I'm lost in its expanse, its metal bridge and concrete paths, the steel shutters over supermarkets and shops. I'm ready to join that list of ghosts, I'm part of them already. An old man on the stone outside his cottage longing for someone to stop and talk, a lone figure on a stick at night following a twisting path.

When I am dead, Johnny, just remember me. At the end of my life all I ever cared for was the sound of your voice on the path down from the road, the slight chance you might call, half mockingly, to drive out the loneliness of those small rooms with their incessant voices. And that after the pain and enveloping darkness I might at least live on in some obscure corner of your memory.

People treated you different when your parents were gone. He could feel the teachers in school watching him, over friendly at times or careful with their words. Only the French teacher was unchanged. 'I was talking to your mother last night. She is very displeased with your progress,' he would roar at Johnny as he roared at every other boy in the class, peering down at them, not even aware of their names.

What state was her body in? He didn't want to think of it, but sometimes the thought caught him unawares. He'd blink and try to keep his eyes open, terrified of the images that would be lurking if he closed them.

Dusty evenings passed in his grandmother's house, the leather bag on top of the wardrobe which she had carried in and out of every house on those streets. A neighbour who is a nurse can always be called upon by those too timid or poor to trouble a doctor. The birth of children and their death, fathers wasted with cancer, old women with hypothermia like shop dummies stacked on the floor after a sale. How much tragedy had that leather bag witnessed? His grandmother had only cried once as her daughter was lowered, then wiped her tears, retired to her bedroom where the oak death cross she had placed in her daughter's hands was hung back above the bed. The same cross her own mother and grandmother had gripped in their final moments of life, the cross her own fingers would clasp when the nurses moved with hushed voices around her.

His mother had died that autumn, leaves deadening the noise of the wheels as the hearse slowed for a moment outside the home that had once been his own. And peering through the car window, past the cluster of schoolfriends and neighbours, he had seen Turlough, old black hat and stick, staring at him unnoticed at the corner of the street.

Christmas passed and the giddy shock of grief. There was just a quiet ache, surprising him at times like a phantom pain. In February he stood in the early spring sunlight beneath the bare line of old trees in his school and gazed at the old monastery where the monks lived. There were so few of them left now, figures slight as cobwebs staring from the windows at the boys playing soccer outside. The monastery had been a fever hospital once, patients wheeled out to sit convalescing under those very trees, staring across fields where the housing estates stretched out now. Old Turlough might remember it, he thought, though nobody else really living now.

The last few drops of rainwater trickled down the bark and dripped around him. He thought again of Joanie, sitting at her desk in the convent a dozen streets away. It was only a month since he had met her at a dance in the Grove. All evening he'd wandered nervous and self-conscious through the swirling bodies under the lights, lingering beside the bank of coats trying to find the courage to ask somebody.

His throat was dry as again and again he walked towards some girl only to move on at the final moment, cursing himself.

And then in the final fast set when almost everybody was on the floor, their movements distorted by the strobe lights, Joanie had just appeared beside him and it was all suddenly easy. She nodded and began to dance before he had even finished the sentence and her smile relaxed him so much that he placed his arms around her waist when the slow set came on. She wore jeans and a blue woollen sweater and he had never touched anything as soft as her back through the material when they moved with her head tucked between his chin and shoulder. They walked out into the night past the cluster of youths at the gate.

'I've no money for a taxi,' he said, embarrassed.

'It would be nicer to walk,' she replied.

They paused at the old wall on the corner of her street beneath an overgrown hedge that shaded them. The road fell down below them towards the traffic lights on the carriageway. In the factory on the far hill a steel crane gleamed in the spotlights through the gate. Ivy had begun to flower on the wall behind them, other footsteps passing without a glance.

'Where do you live?' she asked.

'With my granny. My parents are dead.'

'That's strange,' she said. 'So do I. So are mine.'

Faking an experienced air he bent his head towards hers. Her lips opened and he tasted lipstick and then the slippery warmth of her tongue. He raised his hands to her hips and hesitated, his inexperience found out, until she reached down to draw them up between her blouse and jumper. Through the cloth he could feel the outline of bra and the heat of her breasts which his hands pressed clumsily. It had been raining early on and the leaves above his head were cool and wet. There was the heavy scent of damp trees and moist earth from the gardens and when he closed his eyes she seemed to taste to him of lilac.

'You could be arrested for that,' she said. 'I'm only fifteen.'

After she went in he stood in the shadow of the wall till the light came on in her bedroom. As long as he was surrounded by that scent of trees and earth her presence seemed to remain there with him. An hour later he walked home, clenching his fists to prevent himself from singing as he passed the remaining couples pressed into the shadows of back lanes and hidden corners.

From then on he rarely went to visit Turlough, the old man. It was his mother who had often sent him down there when he was a child. *See if the old man needs paraffin for his stove, see if the old man needs messages.* Since her death he had found himself going back there, often just standing across from Turlough as he sat on the stone on the grassy bank beside the road, but occasionally going down into the small gully where rusting corrugated iron glistened on the roof of the old man's cottage. He did not go there to talk of his mother's death but to get away from it, from the spaces in neighbours' conversations, their cloying sympathy, the way her name was avoided like a taboo.

But instead now most evenings found him with Joanie, their heads pressed close over copy-books and exam papers in her granny's kitchen, and later talking with their arms round each other till her grandmother banged on the kitchen wall from her bedroom next door in the early hours. One clear and mild night in late March they lay out on a blanket on her shed roof, sharing cigarettes illicitly and following the slow orbit of satellites through the stars. Behind them a grey meadow stretched down to the stream that bordered the carriageway. Johnny could hear the sound of water as he inhaled, his stomach slightly sick at the unfamiliar taste of smoke. The back door of the house suddenly opened and they could see the outline of her granny.

'Joanie,' the woman called and then, when the girl stubbed out the cigarette and ignored her, she called the name again with a sharp edge in her voice.

'I'm here. What do you want?' Joanie called back reluctantly.

'Are you with that boy?'

'We're just talking.'

'That's okay. I thought you were sneaking in to your father.'

The door closed. Johnny stared at her in the moonlight. Her face was expressionless, her eyes staring up.

'You said your father was dead.'

'He might as well be,' she said at last. 'Alone in that room. It's no business of yours, Johnny.'

'You mean he lives in that house with you and I've never even seen him?'

'He's a recluse, like Howard Hughes. Now, I thought we came out here to get away from them and be by ourselves.'

One by one the lights went out along the estate of houses across the road as Joanie opened her blouse and then her jeans. Her skin was greyed, mysterious in the starlight before they drew the blanket over them.

'You're only fifteen,' he said.

'I want to be older,' she said. 'Much older. A Victorian woman wrapped up in bodices and stays. Close your eyes. We're lying on an old Chesterfield couch. Touch me.'

After a few moments she gasped and caught his hand.

'Not here, Johnny, not now, I'd scream, I'd have to bite into something to stop myself.'

He trembled against her flesh as she held him tight.

'Soon,' she said. 'It will happen soon.'

A gruff fucker with a goat, scruffy from the filth of the roads. Patric or Patrgh or some such name, prophesying out of him down by the steam. His three gods that form the one god, his riddles and his trickery. Too many bloody foreigners pass this way and this blow-in not even bothering to hawk or trade with us. His own scrawny goat given to him by some raggedy king up in the arse of Tara. The gods would piss on you if you sacrificed the like of it to them.

People are too gullible in this place, taking in every showman and tramp. Baptizing them is what he calls it, his huge feet splashing around in my stream. I've to drink that water when it comes down past my hut. It's bad enough without his dirt and the head lice of half the village. I blame the druids, that lax shower of bastards. The ones in my father's day would have set their hounds on him at sight or cut out his tongue. Down there now arguing the toss with him, their gods against his god, their laws against his claptrap.

There's only one set of gods in this place and any thickhead knows that. Down where the two streams meet at evening, the branches leaning across the beryl trout pools. Often I sit there for days, not needing food or drink or even to shit, not knowing if it's light or dark, not feeling cold or rain. I can smell murder there and that's a fact. And I'll welcome it, just see if I don't. One more face for someone else to glimpse when the water is as clear as its name. Water and fire, fire and water, they are the only gods that are renewable. That knacker with his cross which some foreigner died on for us, it will never catch on here, just like all the other fads.

This morning I wandered into the thick of the crowd. His lips were white with dust, his eyes half mad. Himself and the druids were at it blow for blow. Nobody even saw me slipping away. A scrawny goat but the winter is coming. His master will never find the tracks up through the great wood. I'm partial to goat's milk just before dawn, squeezing the teat down, letting it run over my beard. A fool and his goat are easily parted and it serves him right. The gods were here long before the likes of us and they'll not be shifted by all his tricks and taunts.

Every morning before dawn I pause at this last spot. Concrete and metal between the ghosts of water and me. The skylights of the factories glowing like a distant city. His coarse voice merging with the Abbot Flann, successor of Duibhlitter, Caencomhrac and Faelchu, preceding Fearghus, then Cuimneach, then Bran. The hoarsest of whispers and the faintest, like old machines in those factories, grinding away by themselves for eternity after somebody forgot to switch them off.

Over the days that followed he hardly slept, his grandmother having to force him to eat. Joanie's face came between him and every thought, her voice constantly into his mind. He couldn't bear being in the garden after rain because the scent of damp earth brought back the night they met.

The weekend came and after midnight on the Saturday they cycled out past the final street light, down the slope by the old ruined barn at Jamestown and away into the countryside. The noise of cattle breathing in the fields, the scurry of claws in a ditch, the steady hum of bicycle wheels as they rode through Dubber Cross and Pass-If-You-Can, beneath the single street light of St Margaret's with its holy well and out along the twisting lanes towards the airport. Joanie stopped by the gateway of a field of wheat. They hid the bicycles among the briars in the ditch and climbed the three-bar gate.

With the stalks reaching up above their waists, it felt like being cast adrift in a grainy ocean. They stumbled for their footing and clasped each other's hands as they waded towards the ruin of a tower set on a headland in the centre of the field. It had no roof and smelt as if cattle had often sheltered there. The earth was flattened in one corner where they laid the blanket down. Johnny had a naggin of whiskey which burnt against his throat as he raised it and gazed at the moon-grey crop encircling them. Never had he been so alone with her, cut off on this small island of dry mud and old stone. A wind shivered the wheat. He knew the cold had not caused the goose pimples on his flesh.

'A couch,' he said, feeling the blanket under his hand. She knelt down beside him.

'No,' she whispered. 'A serving girl driving her Daddy's cattle home, waylaid by a gentleman and lured here against her will.'

He mounted her slim limbs nervously, uncertain of what to do next, and when he felt the sheathed tip begin to enter her he twisted and bucked frantically. Joanie laughed and calmed him though she seemed nervous herself, taught him how to enter her slowly and find his rhythm, till he forgot the fear that he would grow limp or come too soon.

When he came he cried out, swamped by the sensation. After a few moments she put his jacket over her bare shoulders and reached down to take an old cigarette case from her jeans. She lit a cigarette and walked over to the tower entrance. The fantasy seemed forgotten. He felt suddenly cold and wanted to sleep.

'My granny says she often sees you going down to the

old fellow who lives in that cabin below the road. She says he's half mad, has been since she was a girl. What are you talking to the likes of him for?'

'I don't know,' Johnny said. 'Been calling into him since I was a kid. I suppose I used to find him interesting, talking about the way things used to be here. He'd know everything about this tower if I asked him.'

Joanie turned and her face seemed hurt and bewildered.

'All that matters about this place is what we've just done here. Before that it was only stones and muck and cow shite. It's our secret now. Why would you want to spoil it by telling some old knacker like that?'

Johnny went to stand beside her. Thinking back he couldn't even remember when he had first seen the old man. Turlough had just always seemed to be there, a lost figure outside the new shopping centre or leaning on his stick at the crest of the main street to watch Johnny march past to early mass beneath the tricolour and papal flag in his green cub scout uniform. But somehow the old man had become linked with earlier memories, standing at the bottom of the long garden with the girl from next door shouting to scare him, *Look, the Bogeyman's in the hedge*. And as he turned to run he had always imagined that he caught a glimpse of an old face watching, shaped out of twigs and crooked branches.

The fact that the old man never treated him as a child had attracted him first. At nine or ten years of age he would sit in the dim rooms of the cottage, listening to the old voice talking about things which had occurred in the village once, with a half-bored and half-fascinated sense of importance at being there.

The two grey photographs of Turlough's dead father on the kitchen wall, the four tiny panes of glass in the thick wooden frame set deep in the narrow windows, the bare flagstones and blackened wall above the fireplace. The cottage was set on a small incline below the road, a useless patch of land that had somehow escaped the planner's designs. Nearby a small stream rushed from an underground pipe to meander its way down, brushing past the gable and on for a few hundred yards through the gully by the playing fields until it vanished again, back into another pipe.

Often, if he was bored, Johnny would stand on the weathered plank above the stream to the cottage and call Turlough's name. He'd balance there on one leg over the water, as if flaunting his youth and energy, until the old man limped out. He would sit inside while evening, through the bushes which tapped against the window, grew dark over the playing fields and the lights in the distant houses came on. Back then he had been excited by the power he felt at the old man's need for company, by how Turlough would invent new twists in each story to spin them out and keep him there.

Now Joanie's arm was drawn around his shoulder, smooth and warm, enclosing him. Those evenings came back to him again, the old man leaning across to whisper like a conspirator, their bodies almost touching in the narrow confines of the darkened kitchen. She pressed the cigarette against his lips, her young upright breasts shifting inside his open jacket. He inhaled deeply and put his arm around her waist. He was flushed and exhilarated after the loss of his virginity and yet felt a curious let-down as if somehow he had expected more. He felt a man at last, his hand moving down his jacket to rest on her flesh. She was his future and everything that had happened to him before this was dead ash which had fallen away. He shuddered, remembering the old man; his dark lined face pressed close to his, the glimpses of brown teeth as his mouth whispered urgently, the red streaks in his eyes, the stubble, the sores that could be seen on his neck beneath the filthy shirt.

'I was only a kid back then. Suppose I've kept visiting him out of a sense of guilt. You know all that stuff about people being lonely and you feel you should help them. But you're right. Don't know what it is but there's something not right about him.'

'It gives me the creeps, you seeing him.'

'I know. I'm not going near him again.'

Matthew was found in that scraggle of water, below the bridge where the carriageway is now. Cigarettes and matches scattered beside the parapet, his old body face down, floating in a shallow pool. This time of morning it was when my father discovered the corpse, fished him out with another labourer who borrowed a horse and cart.

I said nothing to nobody, went to drive cows that

morning in my bare feet to a meadow beyond Dubber. I remember in the field wondering if I was going crazy, the cows shifting away in fright as I banged my skull against a tree trunk to try and stop the words that were racing through me. The RIC from the barracks by the convent cycled round, an inspector came from Dublin in a motor car with children running behind it all the way up the village. They never discovered if it was an accident or murder.

Once in winter this stream used to flood, now it goes on fire on choked summer evenings, full of oil and shit, a tiny current pulsing through the build-up of rubbish. It will be dawn soon, the first cars and the footsteps of the day shift above on the road. My legs ache but I can rest now, kneel by the stream to break its slick rainbow of oil and watch my features slowly float back into being. They blend so easily with the muck now after ninety-two years of washing.

A last gaze up at the road where the first bus has appeared. The driver will wait between stops at the gap in the wire for the men from the night shift. I helped to build those factories when the jobs here dried up on the land. Protestants owned them, there were disputes about time off for early mass on holy days. I was fifty-seven then, hard to learn new skills, the taste of dust and heat of machines after half a century out of doors. Coming home when the girders were going up with the jangle of nails in my pocket. My father waiting for me half blind on the step I still sit on outside. The pair of us alone with the new names and tunes on the wireless; me walking for half the night while he fumbled with his beads and muttered in and out of sleep. I knew he took it bad, the fact I never married. No voices of children, just the pair of us growing cranky and silent like bachelor brothers. Rickets are an awful curse on a man, the legs gone on him those final three years. Unable to walk to the old village they were knocking down, and up the steps to the little graveyard where my mother lay. I went in his place and answered his questions; was I keeping it the way he had always kept it for her? Both of us knowing what he was really asking: would I keep the grave up for him when he was lowered into the soil?

The day they poured the concrete for the shop-floor I found him half on the bed and half off it, his body already cold. He lies with my mother twenty paces to the left of where the old cross was buried. I remember the bus loads of men looking for work as the hearse paused for a moment outside the Duck Inn, the new estates going up in the east as we turned right towards St Patrick's Well. The last of the old neighbours crowded into this kitchen, nobody older than him, no person able to remember as far back. And the sound of a radio in the new houses across the road, dance music playing as each old face crossed the plank over the stream, the darkness of the roadside waiting to claim them. And when they were gone there I was left, never able to follow, climbing up to the road each morning for work, the endless casks of telephone cable around which I hammered planks to seal them off, dreading the call to the office and the brief speech to mark my retirement.

Tonight, like every Hallowe'en, they will descend on the stream. For days now every youth in the place has been gathering the wood and tyres for their bonfires. There are five of them, like stakes for witches, awaiting petrol and matches within sight of my house. All Saints' night, All Souls' and Hallowe'en, the night for ghosts to walk. He took it bad I never married, no young voices to pray on All Souls' as he had prayed all day for his own dead. I have the two half crowns still that I pressed over his eyes. The four candles that I set around the corners of the bed and the white sheet that covered him, grown musty in the drawer.

It covered my mother and my grandfather as well. But why have I kept them, there will be nobody left here to wake me? No bottle of whiskey passed around the room, just the trundle of lorries on the road above and Johnny or the police or a burglar breaking in, overcome by the smell that will have built up over the weeks. I must sleep now and when I wake in the afternoon I feel Johnny will come again, his young face troubled, asking the same questions. I cannot fail them, Johnny, I cannot break faith. How can I find the words to warn you when a secret is a secret and a vow can never be broken? Two cold half crowns for my eyes when I would love your fingers to press them closed. A musty sheet for my body when the touch of your hand could make me young. Four candles for my feet and head when the only light I pray for is when your eyes grow clear again.

*　　*　　*

That morning in April his grandmother found Johnny seated on the top step of the stairs in the woman's house. He was staring straight ahead as though looking through her. 'Is the boy all right?' one of the women standing below asked, and when Mrs Whelan reached out to touch her grandson's shoulder he flinched and ran past her to be sick in the overgrown garden outside.

All that morning and afternoon while his grandmother waited for him to come home, he wandered through the housing estates, now knowing why he felt so dazed and confused. Joanie called for him at four o'clock and his grandmother shook her head, trying to explain what had happened. At five o'clock he broke his vow and returned to the old man's cottage.

Turlough sat on the small window-ledge beside the stream. It had rained earlier and now slugs had hauled themselves up the flaked whitewash on the walls. Johnny stood uncertain on the roadway for a moment before climbing down the clay path.

'You're a stranger now in this place,' the old man said.

Johnny shrugged his shoulders, awkward suddenly in the old man's presence and not certain of the question he wanted to ask.

'Did you hear about the woman and her daughter, Turlough?'

The old man nodded quietly. The cigarette in his hand was held back to front, with the tip peeping through his fingers and the lit tobacco nestling in his cupped palm. He raised his knuckles to his mouth and inhaled.

'I did.'

'Did you know her, Turlough? I mean to see even? What was she like?'

'The mother? Lonely, frightened.'

'Did you know about her daughter?'

'How could I?'

'I don't know. But did you?'

The old man raised himself slowly from the window-ledge and limped through the low doorway without replying. Johnny followed him across the stone flags into the dim kitchen.

'You did know about her, Turlough. Did the woman tell you?'

'Sandra was the woman's name. I never spoke to her.'

'Then how did you know about her?'

The old man moved further away into the only other room in the cottage. The second bed was made up as though awaiting his father's return. A narrow space divided it from Turlough's bed where he sat down, his face grave, almost angry. The room smelt of must. Johnny waited a moment before following. It was the first time the old man had refused him anything and instead of welcoming him he now seemed to resent Johnny's presence.

'What were they doing in that house all those years?'

'Waiting.'

'For what? For someone to come?'

Turlough turned his face towards the wall as if annoyed

at himself for having said so much. He ignored the boy's other questions and lay there, waiting for him to leave. Johnny walked towards the doorway and stopped. Since that morning a buzzing had been in his head, like a fuzziness he could not shake off. *Tinnitus.* The word came to him, remembering the father of a schoolfriend who had suffered from a disease of the ears. But it didn't feel like anything physical. It was an irritation, like when you wake at night, trying for no reason to remember a word which retreats further away the more you try to think of it.

'I felt something there, Turlough,' he said hesitantly. 'Something I couldn't see. I'm frightened by it.'

Turlough raised his head. Johnny hesitated, ashamed to say anything that might seem ridiculous. But Turlough was not part of the everyday world, the old man rarely spoke to anyone, and what was spoken of in that room would never matter in the real world that Johnny could return to just by climbing back up the path to the roadway.

'It was as if a child's bony fingers had pinched me in the back. I felt the hair of my neck go stiff and it took me a long time to turn my head. When I did I could see the faded roses on the wallpaper pattern behind me but there was a small child there and yet there wasn't one. It was as if I could see the outline of her and yet also make out the pattern of the wallpaper perfectly through her. But it wasn't really a child, more like an embryo, just a presence, the faintest hint of features and it seemed to be smiling. It doesn't make sense, Turlough.

I'm afraid to tell anybody else. Am I going mad in the head or what?'

The old man had risen excitedly from the bed. Any trace of animosity was gone. His arms shook as he reached out to touch Johnny's shoulders. The boy pushed him back in alarm, staring at the discoloured skin around his nose, the folds of loose flesh in his neck.

'You're not mad, Johnny, you saw it too.' His voice almost trembled with excitement. 'It's over a century since that house burnt down. Her people still live in the cottages below by the bridge.'

Which cottages? Johnny wanted to ask, thinking suddenly of Joanie, but the old man was rambling on almost incoherently and he couldn't stop him.

'You could still see the charred stones when I was a boy. It happened the year before I was born. They say the woman fell piling turf on the fire. The child was stillborn inside her. Never saw the light of day. Limbo, Johnny, that's where the priests said souls like that go, if they can find their way there. What man can live with a presence like that? Burnt to the ground. Every last stick in it burnt.'

'Turlough, will you listen to me. It's like my head is throbbing, like I can't think straight . . .'

'I know. I know. Johnny, we cannot always pick the path of our lives. Forgive me, Johnny, and remember me, that's all I ask, just remember me too.'

Without warning the old man placed his withered arms around Johnny's shoulders in an embrace that the boy was too terrified and filled with incomprehension to back away from.

It was May when the Head Brother himself phoned the house. The clamour of feet and bells was drowned as Mrs Whelan closed the glass door into the narrow corridor and knocked on the office door. There was a smell of floor wax in the small room. Copy-books and schedules were piled in every available space. She listened to the man in the black robe with the glasses set far down his nose. Walking out of classes in progress, incomprehensible essays, minimum attention span, shivering at his desk and talking to himself.

'How long is the boy's father dead?'

'Four years. His mother sold the house and moved back in with me.'

'The father's name was Whelan too. When I was growing up in Monaghan that was a cure for the whooping cough, to visit three houses where the woman's married and maiden names were the same. As a retired nurse you'd have no truck with ideas like that.'

'I saw women with sick children queuing here without the money for doctor or tablet. They'd have walked to Monaghan or anywhere else for the faintest chance their children might get well.'

The Head Brother rose to stare out between the slats in the blinds at the playing fields.

'Maybe we were all too poor back then, too preoccupied with keeping body and soul together to worry about disorders of the mind. The boy took his mother's death hard. And now the pressure of exams. It's hard for us to imagine, Mrs Whelan, what sort of pressure these young people are under. It's . . . disturbing for the other boys, not good for himself. A few weeks' rest perhaps and Johnny will be as sound as a bell again.'

Mrs Whelan found herself standing once again in the quiet corridor, watching the swarms of boys changing class through the glass doors, and knew that she had been fooling herself for the past weeks. All the winter mornings that she had risen, the list of calls in the breast pocket of her uniform; the black bicycle harder to push with the years; the varicose veins. The thoughts of her final years had sustained her: plants growing in ordered rooms, the scratch of claws as a cat climbed up to sit astride her armchair and the prospect of grandchildren running in, the scent of baking, her smile as they sliced the hot scones open. Nothing was normal any more and the world she had spent her life working towards had been eclipsed without her noticing.

A row of cherry blossoms stood in the square of grass beyond the high railings of the dispensary. He remembered his mother's stories of waiting there as a girl after school for his grandmother to finish her work; the rows of children to be vaccinated from the new estates, the glances sneaked at the boys in short black trousers, their hair cut as if their fathers had placed a bowl over their skull and trimmed around the sides of it.

Even when he had last sat on these ranks of chairs below the high windows queuing in turn for his own vaccinations, the two new nurses had fussed over him because of who his grandmother was. Now he was anonymous, the youngest in the row of adults awaiting medication. The psychiatrist read out a long list of questions, ticking off his answers with a biro while Johnny stared at the calendar with the map of Ireland, from the pharmaceutical company, above the man's head.

'That's what my mind's like,' he said. 'Like the tip of Kerry and the whole of Connacht were straining to link together and yet they can never join up.'

It was late, the rows of benches empty at last, the cleaners chattering in the corridor outside as they started their work. The man handed him the illegible prescription without replying. Johnny stared at the small sheet of paper.

'My granny, Mrs Whelan,' he said, 'she'll be able to decipher it.'

'Why?' the man replied. 'Is she on tablets as well?'

The red tablets made him drowsy and as the summer drew on he began to gain weight from lying in bed until early afternoon. When he rose he walked the streets or was drawn reluctantly down to Turlough in his cottage. If only his mind could shape the question he needed answered he might get well again. Instead, the old man and himself sat in the gloom of those small rooms like an old married couple sulking for so long they had forgotten what they had quarrelled about.

He shunned his old schoolfriends who either jeered or

treated him cautiously like a retarded child. Autumn came and only the gang of youths who spent the evenings littering the waste ground along the rivulet with flagons of cider and cheap sherry accepted him without question for what he was.

'Here's the bleeding mad bloke,' they would say and he'd sit on the grass beside them and slug from the bottle in turn while they passed the hours boasting and cursing and trying to throw each other into the oily water. With them he forgot everything except the burning sting of alcohol on his throat and the harsh raw laughter in which he joined at the clowning of men whose brains had been burnt away by acid and booze and smack.

All the deaths his grandmother had witnessed without breaking. Her husband and son-in-law and then even her own daughter lowered into the earth before her. But that ingrained sense of purpose had kept her battling on. Parents to be consoled in the early days of the suburb, collections organized, children whose mothers were sick sleeping on mattresses on her floor. Even in her own grief, caring for her grandson had been first in her mind. Poverty and physical sickness, these were the enemies she knew. Carbolic soap and plates of soup covered with a cloth, a feverish child to be sponged down. Even after she retired she had never been idle, neighbours still calling to her door in the night. Now, faced with Johnny, she was suddenly impotent, sitting in the dining-room by the television and the new gas fire, her face aged as if all the tragedies she had witnessed had only now sunk in.

Some evenings Joanie still called. She was in fifth year now, impersonating the old nuns who wandered like hens in and out of the classrooms. Johnny lay on his bed while she rooted among the abandoned school books in the corner.

'I know they're a crock of shit, Johnny,' she said. 'But you can't just give up on everything. Do you never even try to open them?'

'I can't. It's like there's a perpetual humming in my head, like a radio that has been left turned on between stations. Those tablets they gave me have only made it worse. I can't drown it out and I can't think straight with it. Yesterday I started playing music at the wrong speed just to block it out and when that failed I smashed every record I have on the roadway. Jesus, Joanie, this morning I couldn't even remember doing it.'

'My granny says you spend half your life down visiting that old bastard.'

'So what if I do?'

'You promised me once.'

'Joanie, I'm frightened of something I don't understand.'

'I'm frightened too,' she said, 'scared of losing you. Whatever that old fellow is saying he's screwing you up. My granny is away tonight. Come over, we'll be alone. We'll see this through together.'

'What about your sister and your father?'

'My sister will do what she's told. My father is in his room. He doesn't want to come out of it.'

'I don't know.'

She gave him a strange look as though reluctant to speak.

'Please, Johnny. I'm frightened to be in the house alone with my Da.'

That night she had a bottle of gin hidden in the bedroom. Meatloaf roared out of hell from the record-player. The bottle was nearly finished before they undressed. He took her with a violence she had never experienced before, on her knees with her head buried in the pillow. He raised the gin to his lips, drained it and felt her shiver when the bottle smashed against the wall. He imagined her father lying there, listening to him. If the man was in the cottage he gave no sign of existing. It was the eve of Hallowe'en. A mask belonging to her sister lay on the floor. The distorted features leered back at him. He gazed at Joanie's naked shoulders sloping away and tried to recapture the closeness which had once overwhelmed him, but all he saw was an anonymous body granting anonymous pleasure. The glimpse of a blue jumper in a dance hall, two heads touching over a school book, the outline of breasts beneath his open jacket in a moonlit field: these were the memories of somebody else, a tenderness he remembered but could not recreate, the lights of a bright ship ploughing towards the horizon leaving him cast off on an island of inertia.

He wanted to ask her to forgive him but when he looked

down again for a moment he seemed to glimpse the anaemic flesh of the woman's daughter hanging like an after-image between Joanie and him, like the indistinct features of the child he had seen in her house. He shuddered and came and in the cold aftermath of sex Joanie lay beside him, her skin saturated with sweat, her arms clutching him desperately.

'I'm frightened in this house, Johnny. My father is going to die on me, I can feel it. He's going to die and leave me alone with her. She's killing him and I'm helping her. I'm afraid to go near his door, afraid she'll see. Johnny, don't go away on me. I'd do anything for you, even have a child if you wanted. I need you, Johnny, do you understand me?'

He lay beside her without speaking.

'What are you thinking of, Johnny? Do you even know I'm here?'

He said nothing and eventually when he felt her shoulders move as she cried he stroked her.

'Why are you doing this to me, Johnny, I'll give you anything you want. It's that old fellow causing it, he's an evil bastard. You were never like this before you went back to visit him. He's destroying you. For my sake give him up!'

Inside he felt as barren as a burnt cigarette. All there was left was pity for this strange weeping girl and an overwhelming desire to get away from her. He began to dress with the light still off and the tiny red glow of the record-player like an unblinking eye watching them from the corner.

'It's like my brain is jammed and nobody else can help

me. Maybe he knows nothing but I need to find out why my life has stopped.'

He closed the front door and stood on the path. There was the noise of oiled chains rattling in the factory on the hill across the carriageway. The small garden smelt of clay and decomposing leaves. He began to walk towards the traffic lights and with each step found that he was crying for a life which he had lost.

All afternoon I waited for him to call, the selfish part of me longing for release, the other part wanting to scream a warning. How many more chances would I have to save him, how often more would my tongue fail?

Daylight was starting to fade when he came. Now he will not come back again. His footsteps crossing the plank and climbing up the bank to the road, leaving me here to watch the sky darken through the branches outside the small window. Would he have believed a word I said and even if I told him would it make any difference? Could it all be a crazy delusion spun round an unjustifiable act in my youth? Was I normal even before it happened? He started again about the woman's daughter, as if she were the only one. What did I know about her, who had told me? I knew exactly how he felt, his face so like my own eighty years before that when I looked at him I seemed to be staring out of his eyes watching myself peering in.

'I keep thinking you're going to tell me something I should know, Turlough. But now I think you don't know anything. You're just an old man wasting away in this stinking cabin.'

He sat on the bed with his fists clenched, two stone heavier than six months ago. Whatever pills they had given him lent his face a cloudy, retarded look. I wanted to explain, to tell somebody after all these years.

'I was a bit younger than you Johnny, hired out to farmers, bringing in a wage. There was one night that I never told you about. My head splitting for weeks before it, afraid to tell anyone in case I wound up in the asylum down below the bridge. My father had sent me through the woods with a message for a neighbour. I knew every stone there and yet I got lost, down below the village where the stream swirls its way in and out of trees. Suddenly I knew fear like I had never known, the very roots of the trees seemed to be alive there, the blind nostrils of rabbit holes breathing at my bare feet, the animals scurrying away on all sides of me.

'My head was filled with the stories I had heard as I crashed and stumbled through the crooked branches. Suddenly I stumbled over a root and fell among the ferns and nettles on to the ground. I cried out as though some beast had caught me and then down to my left I heard a soft explosion of flame, saw the half moon of an old face through the trees as a cigarette flared and took hold. That single match lit up the whole darkness for me. I could make out the bridge where the smoker was and the whole woodland around me fitted back into place. Do you understand me? It was like the man below me was showing me the whole world I knew in a different way. I knew who he was now, old Matthew who lived up in the woods. He was just standing there waiting, as though he had a rendezvous to keep.'

I stopped talking and looked at Johnny. I don't think he had even been listening. His impatient eyes gazing through the window at the people on the road above, coming home from work, the youths passing with their piles of wood for bonfires and the headlights of the cars flashing past like beacons that drowned out the light of that single match from all those years ago. I watched him rise and walk without speaking from this small room and out into the light of them.

'You're a bleeding mad bloke,' Mono said. 'You're soft in the head, you're a fucking chicken, chuck, chuck, chuck . . .'

The youth flapped his elbows and danced around Johnny.

'Lay off the kid, will you,' Git said, handing Johnny the pipe. The stem was so short that his lips were nearly scorched by the hot bowl as he inhaled and held the drug down in his lungs for as long as possible. He passed the pipe to Mono and let the remaining wisps of smoke escape from his lips.

'I didn't come down the Tolka in a bubble,' he said, and gazed up at the rusting girders of the abandoned shirt factory. Through a leak in the roof water dripped in a tortuous irregular pattern on to a black pool on the concrete. Slotted moonlight entered where strips of corrugated iron had been torn from the window frames. Darkness hid the graffiti and faeces and bottles. Their voices echoed in the vast cavern where rows of girls had once hunched over sewing machines. Twice a night a token security van drove through the smashed-down gate, its headlights blazing through the window slats to catch glimpses of lads inside playing football, their shouts amplified as they careered into each other in the blackness. The van circled the plant to fulfil insurance obligations and sped off again. Couples used the outhouses to fuck in, condoms littering the steps down to them. A pusher operated a chemist shop in one of them, two bodyguards sitting as sentinels on the grass outside.

'Come on to fuck,' Git said. 'It's Hallowe'en, let's get out into the air.'

In the car-park four of Mono's mates waited with flagons of cider. 'Are you right?' one shouted. 'Are we getting this bonfire going or what?'

They went out the gates and cut through the last scraggy few trees left towards the open ground near the stream. Johnny felt enclosed by them, their easy comradeship and strutting walk, the way people stepped from their path. Here you were not required to think, here the buzzing could be drowned in your head by jeers and cider and shouts.

The bonfire was over fifteen feet high, a circle of old tyres surrounding the base. Somebody poured half a can of paraffin over the front of it and flames quickly ran up the smaller pieces of wood and along the stream of paraffin to one of the tyres. With a spurt it took hold, the flames casting huge shadows over the grass, the night beyond made darker by the blaze. Thick smoke came from the tyres, the stink of burning rubber filling the air. They passed the flagon round and cheered as the crowd of younger children crept closer, fascinated by the blaze.

Two hundred yards away flames hurled like an angry fist at the sky from a second fire, while on both sides of the waste ground the lights of the estates twinkled distantly as though from another land. In the dark valley by the stream only the single bulb in Turlough's window beckoned. The flames had reached the top of the bonfire by now, the blaze was mesmeric. It caught the faces of the youths around Johnny, made them glow red and unreal like characters from a nightmare. They were shouting and dancing around the fire, hurling planks that had fallen down back up again in a torrent of sparks. The buzzing was growing louder in his head, reaching a pitch he could not tolerate. He pressed his hands over his ears and screamed to try and block it out.

'What's that spacer at?' he heard a friend of Mono ask.

'Oi, Johnny whateveryournameis, will you get it together or piss off.'

'Fuck off down to your old boyfriend if you're going to start that crack,' Mono jeered. 'Our Johnny is a bumboy for the old geezer down there. He likes the bit of rough trade, mixes sand in with the axle grease.'

Johnny stared at the jeering faces, both frightened and yet desperate to be part of them, to vanish into that universe where there was no love or fear, or right or wrong. Just a numb blindness with no rules to prevent you from doing whatever you wished. The buzzing in his skull was like a constant invasion of static. He shuddered, thinking of Turlough's kitchen, the hours there listening to the old madman's mumbling. It was a sign of weakness and shame in their company. That cramped cottage was pulling him down, but he'd show them he was nobody's fool, he'd break free once and for all.

'You want a bonfire,' he shouted, grabbing the paraffin, 'I'll give you one you'll never forget.'

And then he began to race frantically down into the hollow leaving the youths to gaze after him.

'Beam me up, Scottie!' Mono said. 'It's you that fucking brought him along, Git. It's shag all to do with me.'

'Stop up and come on. This I've got to bleeding see.'

For one last moment the flames of the bonfire lit them as they ran down the slope, then it burnt on alone with the suffocating stink of blazing rubber.

He's coming for me now. I can see them sliding down the ditch behind him. How I've longed for this for years and now I'm terrified. I didn't think I would be but I am. Must try to remember everything, forget nowhere, nobody. This dim room where I was born, these clay walls with the sheets of iron that I replaced the thatch with forty years ago. How

I've cursed them night after night when I've sat here with nothing but you cursed voices for company and now they are so suddenly precious.

Damn you voices, if you exist. I've served you well these eighty years, I've given my whole life to you, never broke my silence once. Why must you extract the last drop of blood, can't you let me die peaceably in my sleep? He's done nothing, damn you, why must you place this on his shoulders? All these years Matthew's face has haunted me, the scattered matches floating away as the eyes stared up in horror when my hands squeezed his face back under the water.

They're circling the cottage now, his excitement has got into all of them. Johnny, go back! For your own sake run now! Go back you fool, back! They're banging on the door of the cottage. It's solid oak my father stole from the wood that night the tree was felled in the big storm. I held the lantern while himself and the neighbours sawed it between them. They'll never break that door down. The way they're chanting my name, their eyes glazed like nothing human was left inside them. That's the door to the old hen house gone. Johnny's in there, I can smell burning, hear the crackle through the wall, the roof beams catching.

I'm caged here, caged, I can't open the door. The lock is jammed, damn you, you bastards. I'm going to die in this room where I've spent my life. The bedclothes are catching, the felt has gone up. Help me, help me, I can't go through with it! Can't breathe with the smoke and the fumes here, must break the glass of the window for air. Johnny, forgive me! I never wanted to cause you harm. We're together for ever now. It's got my trousers, it's got my legs! I'm on fire Johnny! I'm on fire! Must break the glass! Break the glass!

There was a spurt of orange flame through the narrow window and the glass shattered as a hand burst through it. The fingers opened and closed with blood spilling from the wrist as the fire spread along the sleeve. And suddenly in my mind I could see inside that room where I had so often sat for hours, the frames of the two single beds with the mattresses burning, the bottle of soured milk on the table exploding, the two grey photographs over the fireplace curling up into brownish flames and then the crash as the corrugated roof began to cave in. And on the stone floor the old figure crawled with his hair on fire, the skin on his face dissolving as he screamed and I could see my own face emerging underneath.

I could feel the heat within the room as I stood in the gang of youths who were shouting. I was shell-shocked, disbelieving, gasping for breath. And yet for the first time in months I was able to think clearly as though a shield had dropped from my brain. The night air was filled with a thousand splinters of wood, dancing like fireflies at the wonder of death. I dropped the empty can to put my hands to my head, and suddenly I felt him, like a scalding flame of energy, rushing out through the blazing door to hurtle into me in a scorching wave of heat that knocked me over on to the ground.

'Why the fuck didn't he come out?' the youth beside me was shouting. 'He had time to do it, he just stood at the window, he never moved!'

I could hear them scrambling up on to the roadway, their shadows grotesque in the flames that were spreading out to ignite the old planks over the stream until it seemed that the very water below them was blazing. And as I turned to watch I found that I knew the name of this place when it was a field, and the names of all the fields where the house now stood, of all the rocks that had been hauled down, of all the townlands that were forgotten. The Scrubby Meadow, the Long Trench, the Bone Park, the Stony Bother, Shallon, places which nobody else remembered now.

I could feel Turlough dwelling like a spirit inside me, and inside him another one and another, stretching backwards in a line from the felling of the giant oaks to their first seed being carried in the wind, to the inn landlord serving the drunken king, the warrior camped in the empty woods, the stonesmith shaping his cross, the barefoot saint with the goat preaching at the foot of the crossroads, down and down to the eyes of druids who turned to stare out through my eyes. And I looked up at the small lights of the houses around me and knew that these were all my people: the woman and daughter caged in their room, Joanie's father coughing alone through the night, the lovers seeking out darkened corners, the gangs littering up the alleyways, the woman's hands buried in the sink of warm dishes, the workers cursing on the late shift, the widower awake in the early hours with only the radio for company.

They were all my people, their stories, their lives, which I could never alter or affect, passed into my care, to be recorded with the tens of thousands gathered from over the centuries. And I knew that I would remember each one, that they would live again for my lifetime in my mind alone, that I would never speak their names or betray what I knew but keep this silent vigil until the time came for somebody to be chosen to follow me.

And then I realized that I could never leave this place, would never marry, would shun all close friends. I was damned forever to be shut out, an observer, longing to touch the lives which I could never lead. I shivered, standing in that hollow lit by the fire, hardly aware of the crowds of people who had been drawn to the edge, and it was only when the sky was washed in blue and white by the fire trucks that I turned and scrambled my way along the bank of the stream, attempting to flee Turlough and the ghosts he carried with him, to recapture the person I had been a few minutes before.

I kept trying to scream but no sound would emerge. I could feel his heart merging with my own, his voice whispering in my mind and all the other voices within his, whispering, whispering, no matter how hard I ran or how much I tried to drown out the words.

In the gully below the village where the stream rushed out again from an underground pipe I paused, choking for breath on the wooded bank. My hands and face were covered in scratches and I tensed myself, trying to find the courage to hurl myself in. And when I gazed down at the water I saw my mother's face and my father beside her and all the neighbours who had died whom I had once known. They stared up at me as if pleading to be remembered: *let us live on again through you, don't cast us into the darkness where our names and lives will have all meant nothing.* Turlough's face was there too towards the back of the crowd. There were faces I had forgotten which came back to me, the little girl I had played with who was ploughed down by the car, the old man with the cough who always sent me for untipped Player's cigarettes. And Joanie's face too, only different, her limbs clad in the drab cloth of an asylum uniform. Nearby, a lean man with a haunted stare gazed towards her as a dog whined at his heels. And in the distance, still only half formed, an outline awaited features that I knew would soon be filled by my grandmother.

A few feet below me the stream was polluted by oil and scraps of debris but just here where I knelt it had become a crystal rivulet. I broke the water with my cupped palms and raised it, dripping, towards my lips. It tasted sweet like clear water and blood mixed together. I felt calmed and strengthened by its taste. The crowded faces rippling into each other were still there when I gazed down again and now I knew only that I loved these people, that I would never let them die. I would carry them within me for the rest of my days and spend my life in this place, whatever longings would consume me, at whatever the cost or sacrifice. This stream ran like a vein through my fingers, its flow, unbroken for centuries, bearing me into the future.

Then the faces were gone from the water. A rat eyed me from the edge of the pipe and slipped back down into the undergrowth. I could hear the noises of the cars on the carriageway above, the shouts of the people walking home from the pub on the bridge. I used the rusted hulk of an abandoned washing machine to cross the stream and climbed up from the gully back on to the carriageway. I joined my people walking in the anonymous after-hours crowd up the steep hill towards the ruined main street of the old village. And all that night I walked through the streets of my guardianship while my grandmother waited anxiously for my return.

In the filthy cul-de-sac behind the pigeon club a gang of youths played cards beneath the single lamp-post, two young girls laughed outside the closed-down chip shop, a squad car patrolled through alien territory. I walked silently, an unnoticed figure blending into the landscape, learning all the names and the faces by heart. At the traffic lights beside the police barracks the huge lorries throbbed, waiting for lights to change. From Monaghan and Cavan they had come, pounding through the black countryside towards the docks. A driver raised his hand in salute as the trucks lunged forward and sped down the brightly lit carriageway, leaving me behind with my secret held like a scared bird whose wings were fluttering against my heart.

1977–1990,
The Crystal Rivulet